Be My Werecat Tonight
By Renee Field
Book Two in the Darklander Series

I0625616

Be My Werecat Tonight

Darklander Lovers

Renee Field

Published by Renee Field, 2018.

BE MY WERECAT TONIGHT

First edition. February 20, 2018.

Copyright © 2018 Renee Field.

ISBN: 978-1393825425

Written by Renee Field.

Chapter One

Armed with her note showing where to meet her blind date of the night, Nora Foster's body hummed in eager anticipation. She was glad she had allowed her friends to talk her into participating in the theater charity auction. She loved the idea of all the proceeds going toward the construction of a new theater playhouse next door to the old cinema she had frequented so much as a child. So, what if she had to fork out a thousand *smackeroos* to get her date. It was all for a good cause, or so she told herself.

Nora had a slight buzz from the three drinks she had consumed and was glad she didn't need to drive her car to meet her date of the evening. Walking confidentially, she enjoyed the warm breeze of the night. The darkness didn't spook her. Just the opposite. Night had always been her favorite time and she always felt invigorated when the moon came out.

"Help me!" shouted a terrified male voice from a darkened alley, jarring her happy thoughts.

Great, just my luck. I'm a witness to a mugging. Nora knew she shouldn't enter the alley but the nurse she was couldn't ignore the man's plea. Still though, she wasn't stupid. Quickly she latched onto the mace in her purse while edging cautiously forward into the gray, smelly alley. The rank odor of urine and rotting garbage assaulted her senses. Before she could move two feet a large blur of fur leaped past her, freezing her limbs.

What the hell was that? Nora managed about four more steps and then froze. A real live growling beast of a cat with tiger-striped fur in the front and a sleek mountain lion look from his mid-section to his hind legs stood over its prey—the mugger. The cat wasn't doing anything to the man lying prone underneath him but he looked like he wanted to. Nora froze when the cat swiveled its massive head to look at her. Green knowing eyes, feral with warmth, seared her. She felt her heartbeat speed up and sweat trickle down her back. Slipping off her black high heels,

Nora took a cautious step forward, gripping the mace even harder in her hand.

Tell me again why I am doing this? There is a man with a head wound next to the garbage dumpster that needs my help. Yeah that's it. Just ignore the great big growling beastie.

Inching forward, she heard herself mumbling nonsense words, "It's okay, kitty...I'm just going to make sure he's okay." *Kitty. Did I just call that prehistoric throwback of a cat, a kitty?*

A resonating growl slowed her movements. Nora knew, though, she had to make her way to the wounded man. Mustering courage she didn't feel she took two more steps, keeping her eyes targeted at all times on the large cat. She watched spellbound when the cat licked its lips the minute the mugger pinned underneath him moved. The creature was most definitely male. Something inside of her instantly recognized male strength when she saw it. The massive cat placed a huge paw on the mugger's right arm. The mugger gave one agonized scream and then passed out. From the size of the beast Nora surmised the mugger's arm was broken from the cat's weight. *Serves that bastard right!*

Reaching the wounded man, she turned all her attention to him. A large gash on the back of his head was bleeding profusely. If she wasn't able to stop the flow of blood he'd die. In order to heal him she had to drop her only aid—the mace.

Closing her eyes, Nora blocked out the surreal scene and focused her white healing power within her. The minute her hands tingled with heat she placed them directly on the man's large gash. Concentrating with all her might her body started to tremble. Pouring her healing strength into the wounded man left her feeling queasy and dizzy. A rough lick on her arm startled Nora into complete awareness of her surroundings.

The beastie-cat brushed his sleek warm fur up against her and purred. *The cat purred at me.* Nora fought the hysterics threatening to erupt and calmly removed her bare arm out of reach of his massive teeth. Its two long canine teeth were something straight out of a prehistoric textbook. Then in a blur of speed straight out of an action movie the cat vanished into the black of the alley, leaving her shaky and needy. The urge to run her hands through his lush mane of tiger-stripped hair rippled through her, searing her own body with heat.

Weird reaction. Must be shock-induced.

"My head. What happened?" asked the man she'd healed.

"My guess is *that* man attempted to mug you. I heard you calling for help."

The man moved to his knees, still holding his head. "Did you do that?" He pointed to the unconscious mugger.

"Nope. Not me. I think a big cat scared the shit out of him." Nora shakily got to her feet. "I've got to go. I'll escort you to a cab and you should call the police. If I were you I'd go to the hospital to get that wound looked at."

Taking the man's arm, Nora's head snapped back to the dark alley. *I could have sworn I heard another growl.* Peering through the darkness she shook her head. A gripping sadness engulfed her when Nora realized that the massive beautiful creature of a cat was long gone. Looking around for her shoes, she ran a hand through her hair in an attempt to get a grip—slightly alarmed with her sizzling reaction to the feral beast.

A few minutes later Nora walked into the washroom at Cara's Lounge, the place where she was supposed to meet her date for the night. Once she'd washed the man's blood off her hands she strode to the bar and looked around. The note said her date would be holding a tiger lily. She didn't see anyone with such a flower so she ordered a cranberry and vodka drink thinking to herself she deserved a drink after what she had witnessed. Thirty minutes later, on her second cranberry beverage a man approached her carrying a box.

"Are you Nora?" asked the man.

Nora nodded.

"This is for you. Sign here, please."

Dumbfounded, Nora did as instructed. Perplexed, she opened the box and gasped. A tiger lily lay on top of a small note and underneath the note was the altered old-fashioned nurse's uniform she had been admiring today at Midnight Madness Lingerie Boutique. Taking out the note, she blushed bright pink.

Let me unleash the wild cat within you. Answer your door at midnight. Your blind date.

Hastily shoving the note back into the box, Nora smiled. *Wow! Talk about a wild and unusual date.* Realizing she was in no condition to drive from both the alcohol and shock of what she'd seen earlier, Nora had the bartender call her a taxi. With only two hours to spare Nora was determined to dress the part. A flutter of nervous anticipation spiraled through her senses, causing her core to heat and her body to flush all over.

Forty-five minutes later she was home. For a second she could have sworn she saw a large creature dart around the side of her cottage-style house. *Ridiculous. I'm just over-reacting because of what happened.* She gave a slightly terrified chuckle when she realized she had no idea exactly what she had encountered in the alley. For some unknown reason Nora hadn't been afraid of the cat...more mesmerized than terrified. It reminded her of those strange dreams she had during puberty when she'd dream about transforming into a majestic tiger. It had been around the same time her healing powers had emerged.

Huffing loudly at her silly behavior she strode up the stone-cut pathway to her house that backed onto a thick forest. Her only neighbor for miles was Mrs. Cohen who lived to the right of Nora's long graveled driveway. The scents of the conifer forest, fresh spruce and pine trees lining her backyard were soothing balms to her shaky nerves. Once she was inside the comfort of her house, Nora darted to her bedroom. Changing quickly into the short nurse's uniform she pinned the pillow box nurse cap into her riot of curly orange hair. Taking a deep breath, she turned and looked at herself in the full-length mirror. Giving a coy smile she decided not to put on the white nylons that were in the parcel.

Not everything can go his way. The idea of what she was doing thrilled her. No one, let alone a man she didn't know, had ever sizzled her thoughts and sex like this before. Who knew anticipation was just what the doctor ordered.

Nora laughed loudly at her own thoughts and then froze like a deer caught in the headlights when her doorbell rang. The sound, startlingly loud, slammed a realization into her that if she answered it she'd never be the same again.

Chapter Two

Hank Bowman was thrilled to be allowed inside the woman's house. The fact she let him in meant she trusted and wanted him. He planned to use her lust to his advantage. The sizzle of sex and unspoken desires stroked the very air around them. Shutting the door behind him, Hank advanced.

"Unbutton the dress." Hank knew his stride was confident and sexy. He also knew she liked what she saw.

Her hands were hesitant and shaky, but he didn't dare help. This was something she had to do on her own. The woman wearing the old-fashioned nurse's uniform was his perfect fantasy come true. *And beneath those layers is a wild feline waiting to be unleashed. She just doesn't know it.*

"That's good. Now I do believe I should check your heart for any unusual palpitations." Hank wore a formal black suit. It had been a pre-requisite from his buddy Lance's sister, the same woman who had talked him, a Darklander werecat, into participating in a foolish blind date charity auction. Hank had wanted to say no but when Lance his warlock buddy and Mitch his vampire friend agreed he had to follow. It was for a good cause but the werecat he was didn't like the restrictive clothing. He had however thoroughly enjoyed having the opportunity to preen his abilities on stage.

Hank still found it hard to believe that two decades ago he'd been allowed to leave the Darklander world to venture to Earth to pursue his dream. Becoming a doctor enabled him to thoroughly study humans and help with his earlier studies into inter-species genetics, which was his main hobby. It had taken years for the Darklander Mistress to grant him his request but it had been more than worth the wait. A world of vast colors and strong emotions had greeted his werecat eyes and senses. Growing up in the Darklander realm had been brutal, but for most of it

Hank didn't know any other life. Except the life his buddy Darklander vampire Mitch talked about.

Hank hadn't known any other colors except shades of gray, white and black. Most Darklander had strong mind-shields that prevented other beings like himself or the magickal creatures on his world from reading them, but not the humans. Once peace had been established in the Darklander realm the standard of living on his home world had vastly improved. Werecat Darklander were notoriously industrious and most members of his home pride had become architects, doctors, diplomatic ambassadors to the Darklander Mistress or overseers of the Darklander elite taskforce—the group of Darklander who strictly enforced the peace treaty the Mistress had hammered out with Earth's United Nations. No human must know of the Darklander' existence. To do so was death to the human and one painful death for the Darklander. Hank still thought it was a harsh law, but that had been the only stipulation the Secretary to the United Nations had imposed on the Darklander seeking access to Earth.

Once again Hank resisted the urge to rip off his tight-fitting suit. Normally he wore doctor's scrubs when he was in human mode. The restriction of clothing always made his tiger side itchy and his mountain lion side cranky. He moved closer to the exotic beauty sitting quietly, but breathing heavily on the hard-wooden stool he'd purposely posed her on.

Absent-mindedly he fingered the black Zorro mask he wore. Hank was comforted knowing she couldn't identify him and that she had no idea of the true identity of the man who was about to fuck her senseless. His hand grasped the stethoscope. He held it poised over her heaving chest, noting with pleasure the pink hue of her fair, freckled skin. The traditional nurse's cap she wore on her head had tilted slightly to the right, making her appear more perfect. She licked those red rosy lips of hers and a deep hunger to plunder them sailed through him. He felt his hair ripple and fought the beastly urge to charge and claim her.

"Is everything okay, doctor?"

Her voice was a husky cadence, a lullaby purr, all seductive healing notes sending shivers of warmth spiraling through his body.

"It's serious. I will need to thoroughly check you out." He grinned, noting her posture immediately relaxed with his teasing. She flashed a smile at him and his cock jumped to life with her direct gaze.

His mother would say the woman was like the goddess herself—Bast beautiful. A riot of tiger orange-hued hair fell in tight ringlets to frame her tiny face, which was peppered with beautiful light brown freckles everywhere. He guessed she was in her early thirties and his gut told him she was the type to age gracefully. The soft curls immediately drew you to her eyes. Green cat-knowing eyes captivated you with their insight and playfulness.

Come out to play, kitty, kitty. The minute she flashed those green eyes flecked with gold at him was the moment Hank's inner cats snarled at him. Mine. Take her. Claim her. Mate with her.

Hank lowered the scope to her right breast, teasing the cold flat metallic object around her right C-cup with detailed precision. If there was one thing Hank knew it was breasts. They were his specialty. Over the past three years he'd performed so many breast implants, reductions and reconstructive surgeries that he could tell you with one glance the exact cup size of a woman's breasts. No one, not even him, would have thought he'd ever get to palm so many beauties. But it was a skill he thoroughly liked and his cats loved.

"Is that cold?" He already knew the answer.

She nodded, biting on her lower lip.

"Then I'll just have to warm you up, nurse." Hank grinned, again attempting to part the nurse's uniform.

Her hand whipped out and stopped him. Her hold on his wrist was full of feline strength.

"No."

"No?" Through her thin uniform he felt her heart beat faster, but it was her eyes that froze him—fear. Stark terror held him at bay. Hank

9

released his hand. He wouldn't push her even though he desperately wanted to see those two lush mounds.

The night had taken an unusual direction after the blind date auction. Having heard a man cry for help from the alley, Hank allowed the werecat he was to take over and it was then he'd caught her scent. All woman. Sensual, alluring healing heat radiated in bright hues of sparkling orange and red around her. She hadn't been terrified of him. Instead, spellbound Hank had watched her inch forward, forcing her own fear to heel as she saved the victim's life with her hands. Witnessing her healing the man had almost knocked him over. If he hadn't been watching her so intently he would have missed the flicker of the cat within her that was screaming *let me out...release me!*

Tonight, that's exactly what Hank was going to do. Let the wild cat roaming within her free. He'd used his cat telepathy to discern who she was and quickly read the sexual fantasy she longed for. Discovering she was the woman who had won him as her blind date caused him to preen with male satisfaction. Knowing her sexual fantasy, where she wanted to play doctor, his beast of a cat purred in ecstasy. So, here Hank was—playing doctor when he usually was one.

"All right, nurse." Hank lowered himself to his knees, purposefully using his wide shoulders to part her legs. Again, a moment's hesitation met his attempt but then he felt her relax, parting her legs more on the stool so he could move his body between her thighs. The advantage was hers now. On his knees he was the one left looking up while she sat poised on the tall stool. She was like a goddess and he was going to worship her.

Hank moved lower. She had a doctor fixation, but his mind thrust had also revealed she felt her body was inadequate. *Inadequate my ass.*

"Lovely curls." He blew a hot breath across her pussy, aching to dip his finger in to see if she was wet for him,

"If you like orange."

Her immediate response to his praise confirmed what he felt. She judged herself too harshly. "Naughty, nurse...are you questioning my taste?"

She giggled, causing her breasts to jiggle. Hank stilled his hands that wanted to rip open the small black hooks keeping her titties from his view. He used the opportunity to leverage his body up so his mouth could latch onto her right breast through the uniform. She gasped. Hank flicked his tongue back and forth over her sensitive nipple and then moved his mouth to her other breast to reward it also. Two large wet stains appeared on her uniform. Her entire body quivered from his ministrations. The cats within him purred. He could see all her reactions perfectly even though the room was only lit with two flickering red candles that smelled of strawberries. An exotic fruit he'd only recently sampled and had come to love like warm cream.

"Oh my. I forgot what that feels like."

"I'm just getting started. When I'm done with my exam I want that pussy cream of yours to be sliding out of that warm cunt. Then I'm going to give you your annual check-up...you naughty little Kitty."

"Did you just call me Kitty?"

Hank gave the insides of her thighs a lick, tasting her heat and unique scent, reminding him of fresh flowers.

"Yes, I did. Let's let that kitty of yours out to play." To emphasize his point, he moved his tongue higher, giving a rough scrape along her wet folds. Her body melted into his touch, her legs instinctively opening to him, allowing him to take her passion-induced scent into his body.

Hank's cock was rock hard, creating a tent as it pushed painfully up against the zipper of his dress pants. He growled. His cats felt too constricted in the suit. Forcing himself to behave, he used his fingertips to outline her heaving breasts. Unhooking the lower portion of the uniform more, she let him part the fabric. Her tiny exposed bellybutton teased him. "No laughing," he cautioned, lowering his body once again so he could swivel his tongue inside her round button. She stifled a giggle.

"Nurse, I do believe I said no laughing. Your naughtiness will not go unpunished. Spread your legs wider for me."

When she didn't do as instructed Hank grasped both her legs and hoisted them over his shoulders. Positioning his head between her legs, his thick tongue gave her swollen pussy lips another rough lick. *A real redhead.* He loved that the triangle of soft curls between her legs was the exact shade of color as the hair on her head.

She clutched his shoulders to hang on. Hank realized in an instant the way she sat on the stool was making her uncomfortable. He unhooked her legs from his shoulders and was pleased when she gave a small oomph of surprise.

"Don't worry, Kitten, I'm not done with you yet." He scooped her up, cradling her small frame in his arms and moved to the large sofa. Lying her down on the cushions, Hank made sure her play uniform parted. She immediately clutched the front, keeping her breasts from him. He smiled knowingly at her and felt her relax when he didn't attempt to move the fabric.

Hank loved that she hadn't bothered to put on the white nylons which came with the uniform. Besides breasts, Hank loved toes. Immensely so. He popped her big toe into his mouth and suckled it, sweeping his tongue around and inside her other toes, pleased with her immediate reaction. She gasped and leveraged herself up onto her elbows to watch him suck her tiny appendages. Her head lowered back and those sweet puckered nipples of hers stretched tight across her uniform. *Toes are sensitive objects and should be worshipped. Especially cute tiny toes that are painted pink.* That was Hank's thinking and he had yet to find a woman who objected to his ministrations.

She oohed her pleasure. Hank felt the cat within her stretch, her body purring into its sexual awareness as his tongue savored the feel of her dainty big toe. He moved his mouth to her other toes, paying special attention to her pinky toe. Letting his fingers climb up her other leg, he couldn't resist running a finger through her now wet pussy curls. She immediately parted her legs wider, an open invitation for oral sex.

"Nurse, I'm not done punishing you," admonished Hank.

"I don't think I can take any more."

Hank knew she had no idea she was purring her words, or rubbing her body passionately up against him, marking him as he was claiming her. The cat within her was leashed tight with sexual want and need and he was just the beast to spur him into heat.

Moving to her silky bare legs Hank applied a dozen kisses followed with small love nips, loving the satiny feel of her skin. Inhaling deeply, he finally registered the subtle body lotion she wore as freesia. It was light; airy with a fruity flavor his tongue enjoyed digesting.

"You will and you can, Nurse. You wouldn't want me to report you now, would you?" *Wow, I could really get into this role-playing thing.*

"I don't want that, Doctor. I would do anything to keep my job." She flashed perfect white teeth at him and he winked. A second later the big toe on her other foot was deep in his mouth. He ran his tongue around it and across the flesh connecting her second toe, loving her moans as he lightly chewed on every single one of her toes. Then Hank worked his way back up her legs to her moist heat.

She whimpered her pleasure the minute his tongue savored her musky taste. Boldly his mouth kissed her swollen pussy. Hank tried to go slow but her taste was like the best dessert he'd ever sampled. He wanted more. He was addicted with the tangy, flowery taste of her cream. It was a taste that was going to haunt him because try as he might Hank had a feeling he was not going to be able to forget her. The werecat he was recognized her instantly as his mate. The man he tried to be was trying to find another reason for his unusual reaction to the wild feline of a woman lying underneath him.

Hank plunged his tongue deep into her wet opening, now lapping the cream sliding out of her cunt up in earnest. Using his finger, he pebbled her clit until it beaded into a tight bud from his ministrations. She moved her hips up, allowing his mouth to grind into her pussy.

She was seconds away from climaxing because he was damn good at what he did. She grasped his head and snarled—the feline within her claiming her unaware. He gave her nub a small nip, sending her spiraling over that mark. Her orgasm racked her and he loved the jut of cream that slid out of her pulsing hot core. And then seconds later she turned on him.

Hank barely made it off the sofa unscratched. He knew his male scent had truly awakened what had been lying dormant within her. Instinct took over as he turned, morphing into his true werecat form. She yowled and screamed as the cat within her finally emerged. She shook her lush mane, her fur rippling into its majestic beauty from the fast transformation from human into a wild cat.

There before him stood his mate. A Royal Bengal tiger, proud, defiant and holy—snarling her displeasure at him. Green-flecked yellow eyes held his gaze. He lowered his head, acknowledging her ownership over him. He waited. Breathed deep, filling his heart, soul and mind with her unique tiger scent. Then he laid down, passively allowing her the right to either kill him or make love to him. It was the most painful moment of Hank's life.

Giving up one's self to another. Allowing his mate to set the pace. Hoping she understood the tiger within her enough to make the right choice because when the beast was wild, it was sometimes a good thing to run and hide.

Nora felt heightened. Feral. Wild. Free. The heat that usually encompassed her ability to heal had changed every cell within her body. At first it had been mind-numbing pain but then clarity...the rush of it changed her. She let it. Let that heat that had always threatened her sanity take hold of her. The feeling was so right that she finally understood what she was.

The knowledge she was different, had always been so, and would always be, did not faze her. She had been unique already. Her inherent healing ability had marked her, but that had only been a start. She felt whole and powerful. Tonight, she truly let that wild feeling take hold and breathed deep, feeling her feline muscles bunch and flex, her sleek coat shockingly soft. Her long whiskers twitched, the scent of her mate stealing into her soul. She ambled forward, her focus on him only.

She watched him acknowledge her, lying down to await her judgment and the female within her preened. She was the dominant one if she let it be. She would choose him, but he didn't know it. His anxiety poured off his coat, his sides heaving as he forced a passive pose. She knew he was waiting for her to make her move. Claim or kill. It was that simple in their world. The choice was hers. Shaking her head, Nora moved toward him, purposely rubbing her body up against his, letting him feel her lust and scent her sex.

She marked him, rubbing her sex-induced feline scent all over him. Then with speed that should have shocked her, the werecat he was broke free, turning on her, forcing her onto her back. His large mouth clamped tightly around her throat. Claiming her. She purred at him and felt his hold relax. He moved off her throat and licked her roughly. Then using her might Nora forced him off completely.

Thinking they were on even footing he backed off. Nora used that time to sprint from the living room. Using her newfound strength, she broke through the kitchen screen door without a second thought. The growl that resonated from him was loud and clear. The chase was on.

Catch me if you can...or if you dare.

The call of the wild beckoned to her. She inhaled the sweet pine and spruce forest that rested on her property and marveled anew at the night's sounds and scents as they sailed into her conscious.

She was so caught up in her new surroundings that she didn't hear him until it was too late. He leaped at her—pinning her tightly to the mossy forest floor. He was angry. The cats within him feral—she'd teased both man and beast.

Instinctively she turned, unaware she was doing so until the pain of the morphing back into human form was completed and she was breathing hard from it.

"Knees. Now."

Hank was amazed at how gruff his voice sounded. He was pissed. He felt like the cats within him just had their tails yanked and he didn't like it. So, when she'd turned so too had he, but he wasn't about to let her free. He needed to claim her. She was his.

"You are my mate." He growled the words in an angry huff of air on her now totally bare skin. Then his gaze got riveted by what he saw. "You are marked."

She attempted to cover her breasts but he wouldn't let her. Hank leaned down, took his time to examine her mark and grinned. "Is this why you wouldn't show them to me earlier?"

She nodded.

"Do you know what it means?"

"Yeah, bad birthmarks," she said, flippantly.

Hank couldn't resist. Grasping her arms, he leashed her to him. His tongue darted out to trail around the two small bright pink paw prints scoring the undersides of both breasts. "You are werecat. Like me."

She hissed. "No."

"Yes. And I will help you discover your true potential."

"Don't flatter yourself."

"How did you manage to keep that mask on?" Her green eyes were full of mischief.

"It's amazing what a cat can do when it sets its mind to it." He flipped her over, pushing her more into the soft, cool forest earth. Using his hands, he raised her hips, exposing her ass to his wild gaze.

"I'm going to claim you. You are mine." His cock moved to her slick opening and this time there was no hesitation. One minute he was poised at her entrance and then next he was buried to the hilt, his thick shaft stretching her walls until she relaxed, letting his dominant nature take over.

He thrust deep, and growled...the sound once again awakening the wild tiger within her. She stretched, using her knees to allow her stance to widen, letting him pound into her, mark her, take her like the wild beasts they both were. She soared and screamed when his hands moved to her breasts. He played with her nipples, tweaking them until they burned from his playful fingers and then he moved his hand lower. Using two fingers he found her clit. He pinched it hard. Nora climaxed, her pussy muscles flexing madly around his cock as the hot jet of his semen poured into her. She milked his shaft with loving strokes, the cat within her purring in pure female satisfaction.

Hank nipped a loving kiss on her neck before he slid his slick body off hers, taking a roll so that most of his weight wasn't on her and they were both laying nestled, totally satisfied on the moss. Complete surreal weariness was overcoming Nora after her first turn into a tiger. Sighing, she nestled closer to his masculine warmth. Her purr went straight to Hank's still-pounding heart and semi-hard cock.

Awareness of the consequences of his claiming her and unleashing the cat within her shook Hank. Raw, evocative emotions surfaced. It dawned on Hank that by his unlocking the cat within her it might very well be the net securing his freedom for good. Taming a werecat was not a livable option. They were both wild, free beasts governed by rules the Darklander Goddess Sakhmet herself decreed at a whim.

Knowing the path, he'd taken led him to this woman caused the man he was to want to flee. The cats that co-existed within him wanted nothing other than to take her again and again throughout the night, uncaring of the consequences. The dual nature of his life really was a bitch.

Chapter Three

The shrill alarm jack-knifed Hank into a sitting position. It took him a full thirty seconds to realize what he'd done. He'd fallen asleep. After having mind-blowing sex in the forest, something he'd thoroughly enjoyed, he had carried the exhausted sex-kitten back to her house and had meant to deposit her in her bed, alone. However, she'd looked so cuddly that the cats within him had insisted he lay next to her for a few minutes. *Minutes had obviously turned into hours.* Hank raked a hand through his ruffled hair.

In disbelief he watched the unnamed woman smash the snooze button on the clock radio, not yet realizing he was in the bed with her. Using what precious time he had, he attempted to climb out of her bed without waking her up. What he really wanted to do was slink away before she could spot him. As he moved it dawned on him. The mask had come undone. It was somewhere in the bed.

Shit, could this get any worse? Apparently so because a warm hand on his back stilled his slow progress out of the bed.

"You stayed. You know I had this really strange dream about wild cats and running through the forest naked. Talk about weird."

The husky purr of her voice woke up his cats and his cock. Rock-hard in one heart-beat, it took more willpower than Hank thought to continue to slide his body out of her warm sheets. The hot scent of sleep and ripe, sex-filled woman snarled through his veins. But Hank knew come morning he had to ignore the beast he was. Come daylight he donned his human side and actually went to work.

Inwardly, Hank's body shivered as she teased a nail down his bare spine. The urge to turn, not caring he was unmasked, and take her once again bit into him, almost choking him with need. But he didn't dare turn around. Thankfully he was saved by the alarm. Her hand left his back and he bucked out of the bed, grabbed the discarded clothes he'd obviously had the good sense to bring back into the house with him, and was out her door faster than a Darklander werecat racing through the wild drákon forests. Hank shut the door to her bedroom before she too climbed out of bed. Keeping a firm hold on the door handle he quickly shimmied into his pants, forgoing doing up his dress shirt or bothering with shoes.

"Thanks again, Kitten. See you tonight and don't forget to bid high...all the money goes to charity, remember." He chuckled to himself, pleased he'd agreed for once to participate in the theater's blind date auction.

Hank sprinted down the hall. He turned his head, catching the movement of his woman entering the corridor but before she could see his face fully he slammed her front door hard, running straight into an old lady with curlers in her blue-gray hair holding out a newspaper.

"Sorry about that." Mumbling, he steadied the old lady making sure she was okay and then he made a dash down the long driveway. Still jogging, he rounded the block in record time. Pleased again with his foresight to bring his car to her place and not give into the urge to go there in werecat form, Hank unlocked his car. He was navigating the early morning traffic a moment before realizing his sleepover wasn't going to allow him time to go home, shower or change. He had an eight-a.m. surgery scheduled and a prep meeting before that so his only alternative was driving straight to the hospital. He was thankful he always kept spare scrubs and a change of clothing in his locker at work.

Trying to find a silver lining to his hectic, unusual morning the skies took that moment to open, sending a deluge of rain down from the heavens. His cats howled their displeasure. They didn't like rain. If they had their way he'd be back in his mate's bed ensuring his scent never left her while plunging his cock over and over again deep within her wet pussy.

He wiped his face, realizing instantly her sweet musky scent still lingered on his fingers. A wide grin split his face as he vividly fantasized what he planned to do to her tonight after she bid once again on him. He preened, his cats purred—for once liking the notion of strutting his stuff on stage for his woman, his mate, his werecat.

Hank knew she thought she'd dreamt last night because of how fast her transformation had been, but he was fairly certain come tonight, once the sun set, the felines within her would ensure she knew what was real and what was a fantasy.

* * * * *

Disbelief poured like a rippling fissure through her mind and body. For one delirious, delightful moment Nora had been comforted realizing he'd stayed the night. She couldn't remember much about the night but she did remember bidding on him at the charity auction, meeting him at her house and playing doctor. She giggled, the sound startling her. It was more a raspy purr than her normal voice. *I must need coffee.* Watching him flee from her bedroom faster than a zing of lightning made her shiver. *Talk about making one feel cheap and dirty.* Nora hugged her bathrobe tight as she answered the door.

"Thought you might be wanting your newspaper before it got soaked," said Mrs. Cohen.

Nora took the offered newspaper. "Thank you, Mrs. Cohen. I've told you before you don't have to return it when you're done reading it. I get one at work. And you shouldn't be walking that long driveway in your slippers."

Nora's house was fairly secluded. Her only neighbor was Mrs. Cohen who lived in a small neat, pale yellow bungalow at the end of Nora's driveway. The area was mostly overgrown with bush and dense trees. It wasn't close to schools, malls or many houses. That's why Nora had bought it. She had always liked the wildness of the forest as her backyard.

Mrs. Cohen fingered the large curls in her partially blue-gray colored hair. "Slippers, pah! Say, that man of yours ran out of here mighty quick. It must be one heck of an emergency. Nice man, though."

"Really?" Sarcasm dripped like venom from her tight-pressed lips.

"Oh yeah, while he did almost knock me down those steps he took the time to make sure I was fine. But I've got the gift of insight. Passed down from my father's side of the family."

Nora didn't have time for one of Mrs. Cohen's tirades about her psychic abilities. As it was her normal quick morning routine had been thrown out the window.

"Those kind, caring green-cat eyes of his remind me of yours. That's how I know he'll do good for you."

A hard lump formed in Nora's throat.

"Ahh, now don't be thinking he's like that other scum you dated. Best thing he did was leave you. Trust me on that one." Mrs. Cohen reached out, giving Nora's hand a reassuring, motherly squeeze.

The last thing Nora needed in her life was another mother giving her so-called good advice. When her fiancé had dumped her, her own mother had told Nora it must be her fault and that she should go back and beg for his forgiveness. The only fault was him finally discovering her two strange birthmarks. After six months into the relationship she had finally given in and had sex with him without keeping her shirt on. His one look had said it all. She was flawed. Damaged goods. Weird.

If only he had known half of the weird stuff in my life. As Nora thought that a burning rip in her mind caused her to vividly recall what had happened in the alley on the way to the lounge to meet her blind date. She'd seen a feral, prehistoric cat of some sorts. Nora gave a loud snort, which sounded more like an angry hiss to her sensitive ears.

"You okay, Nora?"

She took another look at Mrs. Cohen. The baby powder scent she used on her skin along with the pungent scent of her lilac perfume and hair dye caused Nora's nose to wrinkle and her stomach heaved. Hurriedly she said, "Thanks again Mrs. Cohen. I'm sorry but I really do need to run. I'm going to be late for work."

Mrs. Cohen nodded and Nora shut the door. Forgoing the shower, she quickly dressed in her usual nurse's uniform with the bright pink and blue teddy bears on it. Ten minutes later she was en route to the hospital. There was no way she was going to be late this morning. She'd promised Becky, the six-year old little girl who had been in the hospital for the past month that when the time came for her lower jaw to be reconstructed she'd be in the operating room with her the entire time. There was one thing Nora would never do and that was break a promise to someone in need.

After this morning Becky would finally be able to smile, something the little girl had never achieved, having been born without a lower jaw. The cruelty of her birth had caused Becky's parents to divorce leaving the little girl's mother a single, hard working mom, just scraping by. Every penny the mother earned went into the medical bills that must be in the thousands of dollars, thought Nora. She felt a surge of anger at the injustice of the world and a system that wouldn't help pay for a little girl to smile. Could Nora understand the mother's sacrifices? *Yes. I would do the same thing.*

Three hours later Nora was scrubbing up. Years ago, she had worked in the OR as a nurse but when the posting came up for the children's ward, Nora had never looked back. She peaked through the window of the door's OR and noticed the surgeon was already inside. He was speaking directly to Becky but Nora's entire body began to throb. Her panties started to dampen with inescapable hunger and her nipples puckered against the rough cotton of her uniform. *What the hell is happening to me?* Turning her attention once again to Becky, Nora fought for normalcy. She could tell by the little girl's behavior that the surgeon was reassuring her, and telling her everything was going to be okay.

Pushing the door open with her elbows, Nora went straight to Becky. Speaking through the OR face mask, she immediately took the girl's tiny hand.

"Everything's going to be fine, Becky. I'm here."

The girl turned her head and blinked hard at Nora.

"I was just explaining to Becky here that she'll never be able to frown again," teased the surgeon.

He had moved behind Becky's head, talking quietly to the anesthetist so Nora didn't reply. She was pleased though that he'd taken the time to talk and explain things to the little girl. Nora had known many surgeons who simply walked in, did their job and never looked in on the patient afterwards. His consideration and kind words warmed her heart, which was beating double-time. Immediately moving to the farthest corner of the OR, she watched the surgeon's back, knowing he was doing his routine. She'd worked with enough surgeons over the years to know they didn't like to be disturbed when it came to their prep rituals. *Not that I can blame them. I think I'd need my very own rosary if I had to do what this surgeon's about to do. Please god let him make her look normal. I'm not asking for a miracle, just a smile.*

"She's out. Ready, Hank," said the anesthetist.

Nora glanced at the clock. It was twelve pm. If all went well the surgery would be over in two hours. She watched the surgeon called Hank work. She wasn't the OR nurse so she wasn't the one handing him his equipment as he diligently worked at creating a lower jaw for Becky. It was painstaking, detailed work. For two and a half hours Hank the surgeon worked on the little girl.

"Done. Finally." The surgeon straightened, gave a weary sigh and handed his last piece of medical equipment to the nurse who was in charge of the OR. The nurse counted all the material, double-checking nothing had been unaccounted for. With a nod from the head nurse the surgeon picked up Becky's hand.

"We made you a smile Becky. When you wake up I'll come to see you."

Nora eyed the head OR nurse. With her permission she walked to Becky's other side. Taking the girl's other hand, she gave her a reassuring squeeze.

"Thank you, Doctor." Nora looked across Becky to see two startled green eyes staring at her, wide with shock.

Immediate heat flushed her face. A hiss tore from her a moment before his gravelly words of "Oh no" penetrated her panicked mind. She took a step back, clutched the OR nurse's arm in a frantic grasp for support and then fainted dead away.

"Wake up, Nora." The harsh command came from the head OR nurse, who was applying a cold compress to Nora's now pale face.

Nora's eyes flew open. "Where did he go?"

The nurse pursed her lips together into a tight frown. "Go? Do you mean Hank?"

"Yeah, him."

"The minute he made sure you were okay he made a bee-line out of here like his life depended on it. Something going on between you two I should know about?"

"No!" Nora attempted to get up.

"You're not the fainting type Nora so take care. I'm going to pretend this incident did not happen in my OR...you hear me?"

Nora nodded.

"Good, because I like you. And I like Hank. He's our best reconstructive surgeon. Not sure why he stays here when he could make a fortune with his own practice but I know one thing...whatever's going on between you and him, keep it out of my OR."

With those parting words the nurse walked out, letting the OR door swing wide. Shaky, totally disoriented and feeling out of her element, Nora stood and then slowly walked out of the OR.

It's not possible. It couldn't be him. That's too much of a coincidence. The minute she thought that her nostrils flared. His scent. That forest masculine fresh-scent that had saturated her sheets reminding her of warm rain, hot male and fresh Irish Spring soap seeped into her senses. Opening her eyes, she realized there was no mistaking those feral cat-knowing eyes of his. In her heart Nora knew surgeon Hank hadn't been playing doctor last night—he was a doctor. The bigger question was why? Why was a professional doctor participating in a charity blind date auction for a theater group? What was he really hiding behind all the masks he wore?

Angry he had made her appear a fool, especially at work, she marched down the hall determined to strip him bare, anything to make him cringe. Tearing off the OR gown, she dumped it in a laundry basket and headed to Recovery. Before she entered she spotted Becky's mother, leaning her head on her lap, crying softly.

"It's okay, Marila, she's fine."

Becky's mom, Marila looked up and smiled. "I know. The surgeon was just here. He explained everything to me. I can't believe it." Tears were still streaming down her face. Nora took a seat next to her.

"Then why are you crying?"

"We have no one, so when he told me the hospital bill was paid for by an anonymous donor I thought he must be mistaken. But not only did he reassure me that the bill was paid, but that wonderful surgeon told me that in the years ahead all of Becky's medical bills would be paid until her smile was perfect. Every cent I've earned has gone toward Becky. I'm not saying I'm regretting the sacrifices I've had to make but now, not having to pay means we can get a nice place. We've been living for the last five years in a one room apartment. We don't even have a bedroom. Becky and I share the fold-out sofa. This...this will mean so much to her."

Nora felt tears pool in her eyes. A hard lump formed in her throat. Without a doubt she knew exactly who the anonymous donor was. *Hank. But why? Why would he do that?* Try as she might the anger she'd had fueling her confrontation dissipated in one swoosh. Instead something warm and comforting settled deep inside of her to nestle close to her heart. Could Hank really be as caring as she was starting to suspect? And if so, was there a way she could charm that caring emotion of his to focus on her?

"Out of the frying pan and into the fire," muttered Nora.

"Did you say something?" asked Marila.

"No. I'm going to check on Becky. I'll be back in a few minutes."

Marila nodded and Nora gently let go of her hand. She entered the Recovery room. There holding Becky's hand was Hank. He turned and watched her approach.

She went to Becky's other side. They were once again in the same position as when their mutual discovery had knocked them both for a loop. Or so Nora was hoping.

"You're Becky's nurse?"

His voice was gravelly low but there was a definite nervous pitch to it, pleasing Nora. She nodded, while her heart sped up and that steady throb between her legs contracted the muscles in her womb. Vaguely, Nora felt she was missing something deadly important as her gaze took all of Hank in.

"I'm Hank."

"Nora. You know you look familiar to me?" She noticed he now wore blue surgeon scrubs. A pulsing memory of being chased by him, letting him dominate her and her being wild like never before caused a flare to form in her stomach. It was a flare of want.

"Sorry, can't say I've had the pleasure. This is my first time in the children's ward." His whispered lying voice caught at her. She knew he was deliberately keeping his face down to avoid looking at her.

Nora caught sight of his brown whiskered face, the shadow of his early morning beard stroking every instinct within her that yearned to reach out and run her fingers along the bristly ends of it.

She bit the inside of her cheek for clarity and gently caressed Becky's hand. Nora looked up, catching his unguarded stare. She immediately noticed how devilishly charming Hank was without the Zorro or surgeon's mask. "My mistake. By the way, you did a good job today in the OR. I watched you work, you're good with your hands."

A wide grin split across his face, immediately making him look dangerous and sexy.

"I'm glad you think so."

It was a polite reply but Nora sensed the sexual undercurrent of what was not said.

"Well, it was nice meeting you Nora. I've had a busy night and I expect tonight to be even busier."

It was the mischievous glint in his eyes that made Nora yearn to sink to her knees. The urge to claw off all his clothing, strip him bare and lick his bronze skin screamed through her, making her dizzy. Worse, she felt he knew exactly what she was thinking.

"You know it's funny but you really do look familiar to me." Without thought she slinked closer to his still frame, purposely brushing up against him. Again, his scent sailed into her. A rush of erotic memories...of something she had become attempted to surface. Nora shook her head, feeling her long curly hair swish around her face.

"Guess I've got one of those faces. See you later."

He dashed out the door not letting her get the last word in, but then it dawned on Nora what he'd said. Without a doubt she knew he would once again be strutting his assets on the theater's stage tonight. That wild keening within her that beckoned to be released was definitely up to the challenge.

Oh, yeah, Hank I'll be seeing you tonight. All of you and I just dare you to wear a mask. Cause baby, I'll rip that off your sexy face so fast I just might leave claw marks.

Chapter Four

"Don't even think of it," warned both Mitch and Lance for the second time. Really, they were harping at him like two old Darklander tomcats.

"Shut up, you two. I'm only telling you this cause...shit, I don't know why I told you." Hank's voice was a low mumble and for once he ignored the rare cheeseburger sitting in front of him with pink blood dripping down the side of the bun. Nervously, he ran his hands through his hair.

The minute he'd gotten to his office he'd emailed Mitch stating he needed to talk to him in person about last night. While he wasn't thrilled Mitch had asked Lance along he'd dished the dirt about the mess he was in, anyway.

"I knew we should have said no to your sister." Mitch's voice was gruff and dead-serious.

Lance huffed. "When was the last time you tried to say no to Sasha?"

Lance was mad, his magickal energy pulsing around him in a crazed electrical circle he was totally unaware of. However, Hank's cats hated it. "Get a grip, Lance. Your magick is pissing off my cats."

"Fuck your cats."

Hank snarled a threatening note. "I dare you to say that again."

"Shut up, you two. Look, I've got one hour until I pick up Tina and then she's going to that blasted theater auction with her friends. We're all in deep shit but at least you two don't have Lucifer breathing down your neck telling you to claim her."

"No way...he breathes?"

"Bet his breath stinks," snickered Hank.

Mitch ignored the tease.

"So, what's your big problem, anyway, Hank?" asked Mitch.

"My date is the other half of my feline soul."

Dishes could be heard clanking as Hank's buddies digested that tidbit of information.

"You sure?"

"One hundred percent sure. But it gets worse. She's a nurse at the hospital and today after I worked my own magick in the operating room we went face-to-face, if you get my meaning."

"You had oral sex in the OR, ugh...that gross," said Lance.

Hank felt his shoulders relax as Lance's teasing broke the ice. His face cracked a feline smile. "No, you moron. She saw me without my mask on and her cat recognized me."

"Seems to me you have bigger problems than her cat recognizing you." Mitch's voice was flat, his brown eyes boring into Hank.

"Am I missing something? Hank's problem doesn't sound nearly as serious as mine or yours, if you ask me," stated Lance.

"Really, you think so...tell him, Hank," said Mitch.

Hank's cats growled a low, threatening note of warning telling him to keep his lips sealed. He sighed. Lance deserved to know the truth. "When two feline souls find each other, it causes the female to go into heat."

Lance laughed until his sides hurt. "You lucky bastard."

"You forgot the important part, Hank," chided Mitch, playing with his food, making it look like he'd eaten.

"Well, until our souls fuse together I will have to sexually service her but while she's in heat I'll also have to protect her from other Darklander werecats in the area who will attempt to claim her as their own. Oh, and did I mention we werecats fight to the death for our mate?"

"Wait a sec, I thought you were the only werecat in the area. Did you just call her your mate?" asked Lance, still grinning.

"Does she recognize what she is?" interrupted Mitch.

"I don't think so. The change happened so fast I think she thinks it was a dream, but come tonight her cat will attempt to dominate her human side. She transformed into the most beautiful Bengal Tiger I have ever seen. And you're right Lance, I used to be the only werecat. Lately, though I've felt the pull of other Darklander weres who have obviously moved into the area and now I know why. They obviously have been getting whiffs of the feline scent she unknowingly casts off. And most assuredly she is my mate. She just doesn't know it yet."

"I thought she was a werecat."

"She is, but she doesn't recognize the dual nature of her feline so she didn't transform into her baser form."

"You cats are barbaric. You really fight to the death?" Lance flicked his finger, causing hot coffee to materialize just too to irritate Hank.

"Really, last time I looked, warlock, you weren't all innocent, seems to me you've killed a few warlocks in your time," said Mitch.

"They deserved it."

"Not sure they'd agree but enough. Back to our problems. Lucifer wants me to claim Tina, which means more trouble I'm thinking. Hank has to convince Nora she's his other half and fight off other werecats honing in on her being in heat, and you've got to figure out why your co-worker, Cindy, is acting human when she's very much a witch. Better yet, you've got to convince your sister to let you once again strut your stuff on the stage. So, here's what I propose. We strut our stuff, let the women bid on us and then fuck them senseless."

Hank's werecat side purred its own happy answer. The notion of fucking was a nice pat, a gentle stroke setting his cock on fire.

* * * * *

Nora was shaky with need and couldn't stop thinking about Hank. All day her thoughts had centered on him. The minute she had returned home she had vividly recalled what had happened to her the night before. Worse, she knew it wasn't a dream. It had been real. That knowledge she felt to her core, which was throbbing for Hank.

She didn't want to be at the theater auction tonight but she had no choice. Bailing on her friends wasn't an option. Thinking those thoughts, she'd looked at the stage and gasped.

"I'm going to kill him for what he did to me," she mumbled.

"Who?" asked Cindy and Tina in unison.

"That bloody doctor, Hank. There strutting his stuff wearing the tiger-stripped swim trunks," snarled Nora.

"What's wrong with your voice, Nora?" asked Cindy, shifting uncomfortably on her chair.

"Nothing that a big beastie-cat can't fix," answered Nora.

Cindy didn't say anything to her and Tina her friend was too busy downing her drink to notice anything unusual.

"Ladies, are you bidding tonight?" asked Madam Sasha, the manager of the theatre,

who had also organized the silent auction in the hopes of securing enough financial capital to construct the new playhouse next door.

Growling to herself, Nora mumbled, "I am most certainly not bidding."

"Oh," answered Cindy, taking a sip of her drink, her hand a bit unsteady, as she focused her eyes on the black tablecloth.

Sasha looked around the room. "Ladies, come now. This is all fun. The other women love your men but your men, as exasperating as they can appear to be, expect you to bid on them. Please for me and the theatre bid on them. They expect you to."

"Well, they can expect all they want I'm out of here." Nora felt a mad sweep of anger, causing her hair to frizz even more. Grabbing her sweater, she stormed away from the table before Tina and Cindy could stop her.

Chapter Five

Ruffled, seething with anger, Nora slinked from the hall out into the dark streets, not caring in her haste that she'd forgotten her purse or her mace. The moon was full and her senses caught the whiff of a nearby park. Needing the solitude, she strode forward with purpose, not caring that people were looking at her in a shocked way. She already knew her hair was wild and frizzy from the night's mist and no amount of hair product would fix that.

"Looking for some loving?"

The male voice petted her with softness, taking away that burning itch she'd had all afternoon to rub up against something to alleviate the throb in her pussy. She stepped into the park, her eyes seeking the source of satisfaction. A feral smile creased the angry lines around her mouth. She purred a welcome.

He strode forward. Tall, brawny male power filled with testosterone. But he didn't make her burn like Hank. Then before her eyes the prehistoric cat from the night before hurled himself with deadly intent at the man. A blur of movement saw the other male transform in a heartbeat into a black jaguar, sleek, powerful but not nearly as deadly as Hank. And it was Hank. She knew that now. The wild side of her recognized his scent that had ensnared her last night.

The change happened so fast Nora screamed several times before she realized within two blinks she'd gone from being a normal angry woman to a Royal Bengal tiger who was downright ferocious. She growled, giving into her cat that scented death and sex. The combination stroked her baser instincts and then all of what had happened to her last night again crashed into her mind.

How Hank's scent had marked her, unleashing the wild cat she was. How he had told her she was a werecat like him and he was going to enjoy mastering her.

Bounding to her feet in feline grace, Nora dashed away from the pull of death not caring that two males were fighting over her. The longing of the forest, her woods, her home...her sanctuary was what she needed. Fearing she'd totally lost her mind and senses Nora let what she'd become take her where she needed to go.

Death becomes you, Darklander jaguar. Hank opened his mind to speak directly to his opponent. His jaw clamped down a fraction more onto the right shoulder blade of the jaguar. He felt the jaguar shudder but the beast snarled openly, defiant.

Relaxing his hold, Hank let the jaguar jump away. The two cats faced each other eye-to-eye, stretched-tight whiskers almost bristling, hair statically on end, as they went at it beast to beast. It was an ancient choreographed dance of death. One paw marked a movement right, the other followed suit waiting for the perfect opening to claim that final crowning achievement—death. Tonight, only one male would walk away.

She is mine. My mate. Hank was hoping the proud jaguar would listen and bow down in defeat.

So, you are the prehistoric throwback the others scented. She does not wear your scent. She is unclaimed. The jaguar's words were a deadly snarl snapping inside Hank's mind.

Prehistoric throwback. Hank was going to make sure the jaguar died a slow death after tossing that remark. *Others. What others?* He pushed into the beast's mind using his abilities to decipher the truth. The jaguar fighting him was young and a member of a new Darklander werepride recently allowed in the human realm. Young and cock-sure, he had been recently thrown out of the pride for attempting to claim mated females. Why he wasn't killed remained a mystery to Hank. Usually pride leaders liked to make examples of young males who attempted such openly defiant acts.

The jaguar jumped in a startling act, catching Hank off guard. His teeth ripped through flesh, scraping over bone. Hank's cats yowled in agony and anger. The jaguar bit again, gouging out more flesh on Hank's left shoulder while slashing his face with his right paw. Surging up, Hank used his large canine teeth to deliver a fatal blow straight to the jaguar's exposed neck, claiming his life as was his right. The jaguar gave one surprised gasp and then transformed back into human form.

A moment of pity pulsed through Hank. He shook that off.

Hank followed suit; the change painful. The jaguar had delivered a damaging blow to Hank and had he not been the werecat he was he wouldn't still be standing. As it was he obeyed Darklander werecat law and with dignity and respect honored his combatant, watching as the Goddess Sakhmet reverently gathered up the dead human-like body, cradling it tight to her mist-outlined form. A blink later she departed with her charge.

The jaguar had been so young he'd died his first death. All felines had nine lives but usually by the sixth time when the pull of death called, the goddess wasn't nearly so tender with your body. Hank knew that from first-hand experience. Praying he wasn't going to need her services for the seventh time, he felt his body mass transform back into werecat form. Honing in on the scent of Nora, his mate, he placed one tired paw in front of the other knowing he had to cover over twenty miles in his sorrowful condition. The pull to go to her was too strong for his cats to ignore. He could have gone to Mitch and have his friend doctor him up but instinctively he knew only Nora's healing touch would save him and their relationship. He hoped he lived long enough to complete the journey.

Nora hugged her naked frame tightly. Covering her breasts with her bare arms, she let the night's breeze provide a blanket of goose bumps on her flesh. Tears marred her cheeks for some unknown reason. First she'd been angry, then confused and now she felt an ache in her chest that had her worried sick about Hank.

Damn you Hank. She snarled the words loud and clear in her mind and then tilted her head back and yowled angrily at the tall evergreen trees. Then his scent. That wild, forest scent reminding her of fresh Irish Spring soap caught her senses. Something was off though. Blood, the hot pulse of it beckoned her to move to find him...to find Hank.

Without thought she changed, letting her wild Royal Bengal Tiger take over her subconscious. She shook her head and then with a twitch of her whiskers zoned in on Hank. Ten miles deep into the forest she found him, bleeding, his shoulder gouged almost off, a steady stream of blood falling from his matted werecat fur to the forest ground.

Nora transformed into her human self knowing that was the only way to heal him. She had to lay her hands on him. Heal him from her heart. Placing her hands on the heaving beast, she never once took her eyes off his. Even in cat form, Hank kept his green eyes...this time though when she looked at him she sensed the dullness of his life's energy fading from him. Something, or someone was beckoning him to leave her and she was going to have the fight of her life to keep him with her.

Closing her eyes, she placed both tingling palms over the large shoulder gash and waited, letting the heat of her healing powers travel through her body to his wound. Time had no meaning. The night's cool breeze over her naked skin wasn't a comfort as waves of hot energy pulsed from her and into him. She shuddered, the force of the healing such a momentous thing that at first when she felt Hank transform from beast to man she was afraid she'd failed. Prying open her tired eyes, she feasted them on his glowing male physique.

"Thank you."

She nodded, too exhausted to speak. His warm arms pulled her to him. She rubbed her head under his chin, inhaling his scent, letting his hands palm her flesh.

Nora vaguely felt his energy channeling hers, refueling her with warm sexual stimuli awakening all her senses. His hands moved underneath her buttocks, his fingers kneading her fleshy mounds and then he trailed a finger-line of desire back along her spine. A feather-tease and stroke of want, leaving her body burning.

His head moved to nuzzle her neck and then his hand sneaked up to angle her head to his liking. His lips were soft and caressed the insides of her body with warmth. He was tender, waiting for her acceptance. She yielded—opened her mouth to his assault. It wasn't a brutal claiming and for that beastly struggle he was fighting, something the cat within her now understood, for that...she would let him take her. Here naked, with only the conifer forest as their witness...tonight Nora would let him master her as the beasts they both were.

Giving a light lick to his lips, she swiveled her bottom in a sexy, provocative pose and then flashed to her feet. She stood before him finally proud of her figure. The strange birthmarks that pulsed bright pink underneath her breasts didn't make her second guess what she wanted. Nora parted her legs, catching the feral heat in his green, cat knowing eyes.

"You're killing me," he snarled, the sound its own loving stroke against the unsure feline she was that said she shouldn't be doing this.

"In a good way?" she teased, letting her hands trail over her heaving breasts, taking the time to tweak her own nipples.

His gasp, more a growl than anything else signaled what she was doing was correct. The need to please him. The want of her taking this small amount of control away from him preened her cat.

She watched him get to his feet. His long, thick, uncircumcised cock causing a steady throb of want to pulse through her pussy.

"I want to come inside you."

His demanding, erotic words almost caused her to go to her knees, bend her ass in the air and tell him to take her then and there. She watched his knowing smile. Blasted beasts that they were, she knew he had said that so he could read her thoughts. His hand fisted around the base of his cock. She purred. Nora watched him show off his proud shaft, pumping it with swift strokes. He made a move toward her. She growled a low warning, liking that his cats obeyed.

"Don't move. You only get to watch."

"Tease." He smiled and did as instructed for once.

Standing still, Nora focused in on herself, letting her hands block out the fact that she was about to give herself an orgasm solely for the pleasure of her mate. She had picked out Hank's fantasy from his head and was going to do it. Pleasuring herself would help her master her own inhibitions while enabling her to take some control away from Hank, because as a werecat he liked to be dominant in and out of the bed.

Moving her hands to her breasts, Nora played with the buds until they were both achy from her twisting them back and forth. She licked both fingers, wetting them to reapply them to her nipples and gasped, as the night wind picked up to heighten her public sexual display.

"Open your legs more."

She obeyed his command. Moving a hand to her pussy, she rubbed herself. Then Hank's face was looking up at her.

"I need to taste you, Nora. Hold open your pussy lips for me so I can lick you, please."

It was the please; that purr of his satisfaction that did her in. Spreading her legs open more, still balancing upright, she used one hand to open her swollen nether lips. His rough tongue was the feel of heaven. She purred, and the feeling was bliss. His tongue and fingers were setting her body on fire.

"I want you to come for me, Nora. Let me lick you clean."

His sensuous words and searing hot look flicked the wild-cat woman on. Finding the perfect balance on one foot, Nora hooked her other leg over Hank's naked back, spreading her cunt open to his probing fingers and tongue. She clutched his silky mane of hair for support and leverage. Within seconds an orgasm tore through her from his skillful ministrations.

"That's one," he growled with utter male confidence into her core as he gently licked her clean, keeping his hand on her leg thrown over his back so she couldn't put it down.

"One?"

"You're going to come for me twice more before I put my cock where you want it."

She looked down at him and fought the teasing smile. "I am, am I?

His sinfully long eyelashes greeted her with a knowing look. She was on her back, lying down in the moss of the forest floor a second before he was once again licking her cunt.

"I like that you're wet for me...that's a real turn on."

Nora knew if she got more turned on she'd have another orgasm within thirty seconds. While thinking that he gave her pussy a probing, rough lick. She bucked her hips in welcome. *The man really does have a wickedly good tongue.* He stuffed her with two fingers, pumping them into her, reminding her of what they planned to do very soon. *And great manipulation of his fingers.* She gasped.

"What are you doing?" she squeaked.

"Why Nora dear, I do believe I just found your H-spot." It was a smug declaration.

"H-spot?"

"Yeah, that's what I've named it. Your hot Hank spot." He laughed at his own joke.

She couldn't laugh if her life depended on it. He was doing something with his finger, tapping on a squishy spot inside of her that caused her body to tighten like a bow.

"Come for me, Kitten." Hank kept up his steady drum beat; teasing the inside of her, igniting a flare of primeval desire.

Nora felt her face flush. She felt the pulsing surge within her and attempted to stop his movements.

"Let it happen."

"No."

"Please. Trust me, you'll enjoy it."

Utter male confidence filled his voice. A part of her knew exactly what he was doing but she wasn't so sure. His hand twisted inside of her, his finger picking up the beat on that ultra sensitive pad inside of her.

Thoughts scattered. Sighing, Nora closed her eyes and let what was going to happen run its course. Her body struggled, tightening to reach that elusive peak and then it happened. Her body burst apart, liquid warmth oozing through her veins while a gush of cream jutted from her core.

Hank immediately lowered his head, licking her clean, again. The act was tender, intimate and so full of caring it proceeded to turn her on all over again.

"That was—"

"Twice."

For a moment Nora digested his word and then it dawned on her he was going to kill her with orgasms. A truly feline smile of satisfaction crested her face.

"I want you inside of me," she whimpered, in earnest, attempting to draw his head up and away from her sensitive cunt.

Hank ignored her. He blew across her swollen nether lips, the slight breeze sending her senses reeling again.

"I can't, Hank."

"You will, Nora. Again, and again and then I'll stuff my cock in that wet sheath of yours and take you as many ways as I like. Don't ever say no to me." His growl of warning told her in no uncertain terms he was having a hard time keeping the beast at bay.

"Spread your legs open wider for me. I want them up in the air...like this."

Hank spread her wide open, leveraging her legs up so she had to pretend they were being held in place.

"So nice," he purred, then once again ground his face into her very wet pussy.

The orgasm that rippled through Nora was like a flash flood, unleashing something hidden even deeper within her. Hank lowered her legs. Her feet nestled into the mossy forest floor, the scents of the woods rich and pungent as night bathed them with its own power.

"I want you to turn."

"Turn?"

His hand caressed the insides of her damp thighs. His eyes bore hotly into hers with anxious anticipation. "Turn into a werecat. Now."

She shivered. He was asking too much. Too soon.

"No." The word was a defiant meow.

His hand stilled the movement of her leg, anchoring her to him like a leash. She yanked harder on her leg, needing the space to think, reason and become normal once again.

He bounded to his full height, taking her along for the ride. Arms of steel encased her body, cementing their union. His torso, all muscles, rippled with the pleasure of holding her skin to skin. Hot, slick, sex-scented glistening skin. Nora inhaled sharply. The physical ache, the urge to rub her body in one languid movement along his slick body brought her up sharply.

His nostrils flared, catching her desire—the scent of her own wet cum sliding with glee out of her pussy while his cock poked into her belly. It was a reminder she'd had three orgasms while he was still rock hard, stimulated, the need for release beating its own rhythm in his body, which was driving her crazy. She'd just recently climaxed but her body was tingling with warmth, which was seeping into the marrow of her bones making her dizzy with want. The urge to crawl up and impale herself on his cock shook her.

"I asked you to turn. Don't refuse me." His voice stroked the beast within her to a frenzied pitch of desire. Her cunt, wet from his previous ministrations, spasmed with desperate need.

"Not everything goes your way, Hank." Speaking his name was an attempt to take control, assert she was not his to be bossed around. Nora was her own person even if she continually had to fight with her subconscious that was screaming for him to take her fast and wild. She would not budge.

"Yes, it does. You are mine."

"Says who?" Nora tilted her head up, meeting his feral green eyes that were barely leashed with control.

"Me. The Fates. Sakhmet the Darklander Goddess who rules our lives. It's our way. The way. You. Are. Mine. So, get used to it."

Nora fumed. She attempted to wriggle out of his tight hold. He didn't move a muscle. "I don't understand half of what you said but get this Mister. I. Am. No one's. I am my own person first and foremost. What happened to charming Dr. Hank, anyway?"

He lowered his head, his breath rushing out. "Dr. Hank is my persona, it's who I am in the day but always I am this. Always I am werecat. A Darklander beast. Bound by the ancient Darklander laws of my world, which force me to follow the goddess decrees. So, don't think you can charm me because I'm just as pissed as you are with what has happened."

"Happened. What has happened?" Her voice rose an octave. He moved his head lower, his arms relaxing as he approached her mouth with clear intent.

"Fate says you are my other half. If I don't fuck you your cat will go crazy. It's called heat and the Darklander werecat within you will go mad from want."

Nora digested his blunt, curt words and then laughed.

"What's so funny?" he asked, clearly surprised by her outburst.

"That's just ridiculous. You're basically saying I'm in heat and it's your duty to fuck me or else I'll go insane. Really, how much more insane can I get? And you know what I think, Dr. Hank?"

"What?"

The space between them grew. He released his hold and the cool night breeze brought her up sharp, cutting into her senses with the absurd situation she found herself in all because of him—her blind date.

"I think you picked the wrong day job. You should have been a veterinarian because then, just then, you might be able to find a cure for me supposedly going into heat."

"Oh, there's a cure, Kitten."

"Let me guess. It involves you and me fucking all day. Right?" She tossed her head up at him, pushed out her chest and clenched her fists together. She could be just as crude as him when push came to shove.

"Actually, we're going to fuck all night. But tonight, you're going to learn a hard lesson."

"Really, and that would be?" Her anger was mounting, unleashing that wild beast within her, threatening all her sanity.

"What it feels like to be denied." He took a step back and placed a hand on his still rock-hard erection. Her eyes savored the slow movement of his hand as he stroked his cock from base to head. She instinctively licked her lips. A hot flush spread quickly across her skin.

"Denied?" The word was a small squeak.

"Yeah, Kitten. By the time morning comes you will understand everything and this...this lesson won't need to be repeated." She watched him turn, his ass muscles pure masculine pride as he sashayed away from her.

"Where are you going?" *The nerve of the man.* He was going to leave her here in the woods after all she'd done for him. *Next time I won't heal you.*

He cocked his head over his shoulders and looked at her hard with knowing. *Damn, he read my mind again.*

"Catch me if you can."

The rumble of his voice was a cocooning blanket of warmth, igniting goose bumps, causing the hairs on her skin to rise in welcome. He turned into his true werecat form and with one leap was engulfed in the thicket of the dark forest.

Nora stood there for a minute realizing he meant what he'd said. Erotic images of what he wanted to do with her were being telepathically channeled to her, leaving her panting with need.

That's not playing fair. She hissed. Mad at herself and hating her body's reaction that was visibly shaking with a mad rush of desire for him.

By morning you will turn into your true werecat form and be mine. Never say no to me again.

His smug declaration was the drench of cool water she needed. Reason and common sense asserted its head, reassuring her what he'd said was mere macho bluster. Huffing at herself, Nora turned in the opposite direction, attempting to zone in on a familiar scent so she could return home.

Once home she was going to take a long, hot, vanilla-scented bath and scrub off Hank's scent. Then she'd be rid of him for good.

What utter nonsense. Me in heat. How ridiculous is that? Her foot snagged on a tree branch but instead of falling on her face her hands instinctively braced her body. Normally she'd have fallen face first into the dirt. The feline pose she found herself in slightly amused her while also alarming her.

The wind buffeted the trees around her. Her nostrils flared and she gasped. Her heart thundered wildly in her chest. Hank's utterly masculine werecat scent sailed into every gasping cell in her body. Groaning, Nora stumbled to her feet. Dizzy with want, she forced her limbs to move as far as possible away from Hank's scent. It was the hardest thing she'd ever done but it had to be.

There was no way she was going to let his cat dominate her. *Cat? Did I just say that? Cats make me think of cute, cuddly kittens. There is nothing kitten-like about Hank. One stroke and he is liable to bite you or worse, seduce you to death.* Striding with more purpose she put one foot after the other. His growl caused all the sleeping birds to flee for their lives.

Ignoring the power of his ferocious cry, Nora ran like a mad woman through the forest, more afraid of what he was capable of unleashing within her than the man himself.

Chapter Six

Nora's body was on fire. Achy. Desperate for relief. Her cunt was swollen, and she felt like she was leaving a trail of lust-coated pussy juice everywhere she went. Primitive instinct, that wild part of her she'd been fighting all night, was winning. Slowly but painfully she was going insane with desire. At this point she'd fuck about anything. The raw knowledge of how base she'd become wasn't sitting well with her.

I'm a good person. I'm a healer. I am not some sex fiend. Repeating the words to her self wasn't offering her any relief.

An hour ago, she'd had to strip bare. Walking for over thirty minutes through the dark woods with Hank's erotic thoughts, scent and possessive growl trailing her had been unbelievably hard. Once home she'd immediately plunged into a hot, vanilla-scented bubble bath only to have her body spasm with shaky need as an intense climax tore through her from the mind-shattering erotic vision Hank had sent her way. The vision had a lot to do with hot water. The feel of him, all hard and slick from the water forcing her to her knees while he pounded his cock inside of her cunt was a vision her body purred for. The resonating growl that had erupted from her throat while her body had climaxed had caused her to leap from the bath, startled, shaky and mad as a hell-cat at him.

Donning her bathrobe for comfort hadn't been a wise move, either. The silky feel of the material scraping over her ultra-sensitive skin made her breasts swell with need. Giving into the primeval urge to be in the buff she walked around her own house feeling like a caged lion.

Her fingers absentmindedly slid over her skin, a sensual caress fueling the need to masturbate.

"Don't even think it!" Hank growled the words after breaking down her back door.

"You could have knocked."

"Would you have let me in?"

Nora shook her head. "No way."

"That's what I thought, Kitten."

He marched to her, his body still naked but a shiny sheen of sweat coated his skin, making him appear even more ferocious and utterly male. That fresh masculine crisp soap-like scent wafted around him.

Nora found herself sauntering over to meet him. The urge to rub her body shamelessly up and all over his pounded into her. The need to mark him as hers ran circles through her rational mind. She shook her head, in an attempt for clarity.

He grasped her forearms and before she could wonder what he was doing her arms were tied behind her head.

Nora laughed.

"Something you find amusing?"

His green eyes were all possessive male heat. Her laughter died in her throat. "Just wondering where you found the rope. You know me, the ever-practical nurse."

Giving a final yank to her bounds, he lowered his head so that his mouth was a fraction of an inch from hers. She wet her lips, instinctively welcoming his. He didn't budge. "It always amazes me what one can find in the woods." His words were hard, sarcastic and edgy. Gone was the playful Hank she liked. The one currently ushering her to the sofa had built a barrier around himself and that terrified Nora ever so slightly to further fuel the needy cat within her.

She let him push her to a sitting position. "Why are you doing this?"

"You need to learn this lesson once. I asked you to turn into your true werecat form and you refused me. I don't like to be refused. I'm your mate. You will obey me."

This time Nora looked at Hank for a full minute before she burst out laughing in earnest. "Remind me again what planet you grew up on? Last I looked He-man went out of style when we moved out of caves," said Nora.

"I grew up in the Darklander realm and trust me He-man is never out-dated."

His pointed stare ignited raw goose bumps of desire as he pried open her legs. Alarm skirted to life. His strong legs kept her from closing hers. She felt exposed and vulnerable to his heated gaze.

The feel of his warm fingers sliding up from her knee to her swollen cunt gave her pause. *Maybe relief is in sight.*

"When I'm done with you, you will beg for my cock and then change for me."

It wasn't a question. It was a bold statement of intent. She shook her head, feeling her hair come alive to the captivating, sensual tease of his fingers sliding in a thoroughly slow fashion to her pussy. Hank leaned forward. His hot breath blew on each of her puckered nipples causing them to jut forward, seeking his mouth. He grinned. She mewed, hating her body's reaction. Her eyes closed.

"Open your eyes, Nora."

They flew open. He was now standing holding his cock in one hand. It was a breath away from her budded nipple. She arched into him. He took her offering, rubbing his shaft around her tight nipple, letting his cum, his scent, mark her. The knowledge that it was his right rubbed her slightly wrong. *I shouldn't be allowing this or enjoying it.*

Still, when he moved to repeat his actions with her other nipple she couldn't stop her body from swaying even more into his rock-hard cock. Hank moved from one breast to the other, from one peaked nipple to the other to repeat his actions over and over again, making her chest slick and sticky with his essence. It was such an erotic play to her senses she felt her legs opening wider, her hips tilting up off her own sofa, her cum leaking out of her. She was in a desperate state. The need for his cock to be wedged tight within her pussy was now a furious inferno she felt from her clenching womb to her achy nipples.

"Do you want something, Nora?" His voice was hypnotizingly sensual. A complete male caress of need, lust and sex wrapped around her.

"I want you." *Is that throaty purr coming from me?*

Her body tingled with desperation to break free from her bounds. There was a part of Nora urging her to give into his demands, change; let that wild feline beast living within her free. That terrified her. It shocked her more than changing into what she had already become. A Royal Bengal Tiger. To change into what he became—a werecat—she wasn't so sure her sanity would last.

He slapped his cock to her nipples. She bit her lips with the purr of how good it felt.

"I want my cock inside of you Nora, but are you ready to change?"

She forcibly shook her head. "No. I can't. You're asking too much."

"You can. And you will."

Hank took her legs in his hands, yanking them over his shoulders. To say she felt vulnerable before was ridiculous. Finding herself in this new pose left her pussy entirely exposed to his feral cat-eyes. His nostrils flared as he inhaled her sex-scent. He grinned, knowing she was desperate for relief.

Then he did the most wickedly erotic thing to her. He simply blew on her cunt. His hot breath washed over her slick opening, causing her to buck her hips up in welcome. Then he'd back off, letting the air from the living room force her passion to cool ever so slightly. Over and over again he repeated the sweet, teasingly erotic torture—hot breath tickling her cunt to the point of it almost spasming with an orgasm, only to have him back off, her body shaking with a fever that left her panting.

A surging, mounting anger over his deliberate actions was rearing its ugly head. However, the minute her anger took hold of her passion, a finger of his would dip daringly to give her soaking wet cunt a slow pass. Just one pass. Hank never dipped his finger inside her sheath; instead he trailed it over her swollen lips. Nora couldn't take it anymore. Tears

48

swamped her eyes. The ache within her blossomed like a hot desert wind, whipping her into a blazing frenzy of primitive need.

"Turn."

His one demand snapped something amazingly terrifying within her. She growled, hurling herself at him in one fluid leap, morphing into what he wanted, breaking free of her bounds. For that alone she was going to kill him.

Hank was alive only because he'd caught the sharp tang of her change. The fact that her arms had been bound was also a blessing, he thought. He too had turned, allowing the werecat he was to finally breathe in her sex-scent. His fur rippled with pleasure. There before him growled his mate. Her chest was heaving from the fast morphing of her cells but she wasn't backing down. Hank was proud of her.

Nora panted deep, the shock of the change into her true werecat form leaving her slightly vulnerable. Hank could visualize the cogs of her mind trying to rationalize how she was able to change from human to a Royal Bengal Tiger and now to this—a majestic werecat. *My werecat. My mate. Mine.*

He silently pawed forward, carrying more of his weight on his hind legs to ensure she knew he was prepared to leap if she went for the kill. He knew it was in her to take him down, but Hank was praying that the healer also inherent in her genetic make-up would overrule her lust for revenge.

Hank watched Nora's fur ripple. She was the direct opposite to him. Marked as his by the Goddess Sakhmet, and he was going to take her. Not nearly as large as him, she wore her mountain lion look, with the sleek sable brown markings on her face. Her back was lined with tiger stripes.

Cautiously nudging her still-heaving sides, he let his familiar scent seep into her. Turning his large head slightly, he let his tiger mane caress her face. Her whiskers twitched. It was the only sign of warning Hank caught before she ran away, once again. The minute he felt her muscles bunch he drew back, allowing her to flee out the door he'd broken down. Hank gave her a good minute of freedom before he took after her. He growled, knowing full well she was going to both hear him and feel his possessive streak.

Once again with the call of the forest surging through his senses Hank pursued what was rightfully his—Nora. Part of him wished she'd stop fighting what was inevitable, but the man he could be realized all the changes she'd undergone within the last two days were far too fast for her human mind to accept. Challenging her preconceived notions of what she thought she'd been all her life was shaking her to the core. Of that Hank had no doubt.

Recalling the first time he'd changed into a werecat made him realize he'd been lucky. When the change had come his mother had been the one to answer all his questions, because unbeknownst to him he'd been sheltered and living in a pride. Werecat families were matriarchal and it was the ruling female who chose a mate, after the males competed for her affection. However, once a werecat scented his other half and claimed her in all ways as his, they were mated for life. But these days it was rare to discover a true werecat, like him.

His mother had been mated with a dozen felines over the centuries but she herself had never been claimed by another like her—a full werecat. Hank was her first born and she'd been proud of the fact he too was like her, a werecat, marked as two felines but existing as one. While his mother could transform like Nora into that of one feline, a graceful mountain lion, Hank was only able to turn into a werecat.

Padding softly over the dewy wet moss on the forest ground, Hank stopped. Observing Nora in werecat form was truly a humbling experience for him. She was dipping her two front paws gently into a small pond she'd been lured to. The scent of fresh water was a powerful smell for a werecat. He stopped himself from laughing. As a werecat her dual feline natures were testing her. The mountain lion half of her wasn't keen on stepping into the fresh pond, while the tiger part of her was urging her to leap without thinking. The sway of her tiger-striped tail was hypnotizing.

A slight night breeze gave him away. She turned; her large mountain-lion eyelashes cast down in such a serious flirtatious way that he purred as he advanced. Knowing he shouldn't, Hank couldn't help himself. The minute her tiger tail playfully swatted him he used his brute strength to push her into the pond.

A growl of outrage swiftly followed. A dripping wet werecat who was obviously pissed off at him wasn't a good thing. Moving his body into the pond he padded over to her, ensuring he ended up just as wet. Then in one heartbeat Hank willed the turn, forcing the werecat he was to change into a man. A second later Nora, in her naked human form stood shaking before him.

"I can't believe you did that to me." Her hair was still dripping wet, clinging to her face, even after the turn.

Needing to touch her, Hank grasped her arms, hauling her to him, warming up the water with their passion. This time she didn't resist. Using his hand, he tilted her head up to his and then kissed her with all the passion that said she was his, for now, for ever and always. A moment's hesitation met his advance but then Nora was twining her arms around his neck. Scooping her up into his arms Hank made his way to the shore, never once breaking contact with her moist, kissable lips.

With his feet firmly back on the forest ground he lowered her to the mossy forest blanket. She spread her legs for him, nudging him with her feet exactly where he wanted to go. Finally breaking the kiss, they both took a deep breath. Hank used that time to study Nora's face. Her green cat eyes took his breath away. She was purity, and a true sex kitten.

"Hank please, please take me." The throaty purr coming from Nora sent shivers of delight all over Hank's skin.

Moving to nuzzle her exposed neck, he nipped his way to her sensitive earlobes. Kissing first one ear and then the other he whispered, "Nora, I'm not going to fuck you. Tonight, I'm going to make love to you. You are mine." Hank couldn't resist growling the word mine one last time.

"Just do it. I'm yours."

She breathed her answer into his ear and all reasoning fled. Grasping his cock with one hand, Hank stroked it over her wet pussy. Then without any more fanfare he plunged his shaft deep into her welcoming cunt. *Home.* That one word aptly described how Hank felt as he pumped all his love into his mate.

Nora's legs snaked up to hug his ass. He loved how she gave herself up to the passionate part of her nature. Her heels dug deeply into each buttock as he pistol-thrust into her. Her inner muscles clamped around his cock with each penetration. Her nails were leaving long scratch furrows down his back and he couldn't have been happier. Moving a hand to cup her ass he leveraged her hips up more, forcing her to take his cock deep into her tight sheath. She whimpered as the coming orgasm gripped her. Mighty pleased he'd lasted as long as he had, Hank finally sought his own release, ensuring every speck of his cum stayed deep inside of her while her cunt muscles milked his still-hard shaft. He felt her purr of satisfaction, knowing he was instinctively answering with his own.

Her hands caressed his back, keeping him skin tight to her slick form. She nuzzled his neck, licking the salty sweat as her legs moved up and down his calf muscles. The sultry movements woke his werecat side up, urging him to claim her again. Not wanting to argue with himself, he decided that with daylight still hours away, the cats they were might as well play.

Sliding his hard cock out of her cunt, she mewled wanting him to stay where he was. Giving her pouty lips a ferocious kiss, he slowly made his way down her body, taking the time to kiss all those special spots he thoroughly liked to lick. Those spots included the sensitive tips of her nipples, the undersides of her breasts, the sides of her taut belly and especially her tiny bellybutton. Moving even further Hank made his way down her calf until he found her foot and tiny toes. Alternating between licking her toes and then sucking on them, Nora became a mindless sex-starved woman all over again.

"Please, please Hank."

Liking his affect on her, he made his way up to her core. Using his hands, he spread her thighs even further apart. With one rough tongue he tasted their combined passion and growled in delight. She purred in ecstasy. Sliding his tongue into her cunt he lapped up their combined cum. Zoning in on her pebbled nub he gave it a small, soft lick causing her to leverage herself up off the mossy blanket as another orgasm tore through her. The minute the sensations quieted Hank turned Nora around so that she was on her knees, her ass slightly raised to his desire.

She turned her head, a question firing her eyes. He grinned cat-like a second before he plunged his cock into her welcoming pussy. She growled her own desire, meeting him thrust for thrust, on her knees, letting him pound his cock into her until his balls slapped up against her ass. Placing a demanding arm around her middle Hank leveraged her body up more, the need to fully imprint her as his taking over all sanity. He felt her cunt muscles relaxing, allowing him to flex and thrust as deeply as he wanted into her. Knowing he was truly pushing her boundaries he kept at it, until her body was once again on that precipice, ready to freefall into a shattering orgasm.

The moment had come. To truly claim Nora as his he needed her to once again turn into her true werecat form, now. They needed to mate as werecats. Telepathically pushing his thoughts into her, he felt a moment of hesitation meet his mind.

"Don't fight me on this. You must. We must. It's our way. When I say, 'turn,' you need to obey."

He kissed her neck, taking the time for her to fully digest his words. Searching her mind, he found his answer.

Turn.

The passion that stole through both of them was blazing hot. The turn was like nothing Hank had ever encountered before. As mated beings, they morphed from humans to their true werecat forms fusing their bodies and minds. Her thoughts to his. His thoughts to her. It truly was a soul-shattering experience.

With his cock still deeply seated inside Nora's pussy, Hank let his baser instincts take over. Pinning her down he bit her neck, a love bite that said to all she was his. Thrusting deeply into her they came together, the orgasm sweeping through them both until they lay in werecat form panting from spent desires.

A raspy voice broke through their thoughts, causing both Hank and Nora to turn back into humans.

"You are now werecats mated for life. His to yours...yours to his. You have my blessing to begin your own pride. Not that you took the time to ask my permission," hissed the one voice Hank was hoping never to hear again.

"Who are you?" asked Nora.

"I, my dear am the Goddess Sakhmet. I seriously thought you'd never let that werecat side of you out. Good thing I sent Hank here to find you."

"What?" said both Hank and Nora.

"You did not," said Hank, knowing it wasn't wise to argue with a goddess, especially Sakhmet, but he couldn't help being mystified.

"Of course, I did. If I left all this up to you and her..." The goddess Sakhmet, dressed regally in a black formal gown that swept to her feet, was currently in her Egyptian phase. Two gold slanted eyes belonging to the Abyssinian royal cat stared hard at Hank and Nora.

"Well, you both needed a push in the right direction. Now, you may approach and kiss my royal feet."

Hank knew this was part of the bonding ceremony after the goddess blessed you but it didn't feel at all that way to him and he highly suspected Nora was about to laugh. Laughing at Sakhmet wouldn't do.

"You really don't need to do this."

"Of course, I do, Hank. She is your other half. You are hers. I have melded you together as one. I have already petitioned the Darklander Council to grant you a special human marriage license."

Nora turned, giving him a nervous look. "What is she talking about?"

"Pay attention. I have gifted you with being a true werecat. The cat was born within you when you were born. I marked you with the gift. It's a special blessing. You are the first human I have bestowed this gift to."

Nora immediately placed her hands over the two paw prints under her breasts.

"It's not every day I create a true Darklander werecat on Earth, so consider yourself blessed."

"Blessed," hissed Nora.

"Do not take that tone of voice with me, child. I am not to be trifled with. While I understand your transformation has been rapid, the time was drawing near. I but pushed Hank into your path. The rest as you would say was chemistry," said the goddess.

"Chemistry?" squeaked Nora.

"Hank, I sense she is not accepting of my gift. That does not please me. The choice is hers. She either claims my blessing truly or I will deem her fit to stay in one feline form forever. You have one night to show me my gift is worthy. When I return, my judgment will be final."

That dramatic statement was followed with a hot gust of wind as the Goddess Sakhmet blasted herself away.

"Did I just piss off a real Goddess?"

Running a hand through his still-tousled hair, Hank mumbled, "You have no idea what you've done."

"For once you're correct. I have no idea what she was talking about."

Hank turned, gripped her forearms in his and locked eyes with her. "Nora, the Goddess Sakhmet just gave you a true ultimatum. You either accept what you are, and honor her customs or she will turn you into a feline...a cat for good."

"You can't be serious."

"Like any cat, the Goddess Sakhmet does not take kindly to having her tail yanked. Sadly, this is one cat I can't save you from."

Fear flickered to life in Nora's eyes. He watched her swallow. "Tell me what to do."

Hank felt his own fear claw at him. The emotion left him feeling raw and vulnerable. Pulling her tighter to him, he wrapped his arms around her giving her comfort, realizing that was all he could offer.

He'd fight a dozen werecats and die a dozen deaths if he could make Nora realize the only way to change Sakhmet's mind was to embrace the werecat side of herself—the side she was terrified of. The side binding her and him to whatever punishment the Darklander Goddess meted out. Mated for life, Hank knew he'd share Nora's punishment and the idea of becoming an average feline, a mere house cat, caused him to growl.

"I take it you've got no words of wisdom," said Nora.

"Nora, when it comes to Sakhmet, actions speak louder than words. She's going to be watching you and you've got less than one day to convince her you embrace her blessing wholeheartedly."

"But I didn't ask for this blessing."

"Unless you want to be turned into a stray right this moment, I'd keep those thoughts to yourself. Let's head back to your house."

She nodded. With a sense of doom hanging over both of their heads they made their way back to Nora's house.

"Can't I just apologize to her?"

"I think you're going to need to beg for her understanding and Sakhmet isn't the most liberal-minded Goddesses." Hank moved them to her living room, where all of what had happened tonight had started.

"Okay, here's what I need to know. Everything. You and I are going to go to bed and spend the rest of the night talking. You, Mister are going to tell me everything there is to know about being a werecat because I know nothing, and what exactly is this Darklander world you mentioned. In the past two days everything I thought I knew has been thrown out the window. And to top off my train-wreck of a life, I've just managed to piss off a real goddess. Maybe if I learn more about this *blessing* I will be able to embrace it."

Hank stood still. This was the woman he'd seen in the alley a night ago—fearless, courageous and willing to take on a Darklander werecat like himself to save an innocent. In this case that innocent person was her. Hank grinned, feeling a burst of confidence that they could tackle what the goddess had thrown their way.

"Isn't the Goddess Sakhmet the god of the dead?"

That one question coming out of Nora's mouth deflated his high. In less than twenty-four hours he had to teach her everything there was to know about Darklander werecat history, folklore, culture and customs. Hank wished he'd studied ancient history instead of going into medicine. It would have made things a lot easier.

"I think we're going to need lots of coffee to make it through the night. You go get comfortable and I'll make us some. Do you have cream?"

She grinned. He wished she hadn't. That one flash of her white teeth made him think of sex and they really didn't have time for that. Or did they? Hank eyed her large bed, deciding caffeine really was overrated.

Chapter Seven

"I can't believe you dragged me here, again. I don't want to be here and you two resorted to blackmail to get me to come with you." Nora knew she was whining but she felt totally drained after all that had happened to her over the past three days.

"Look, we don't want to be here either but those men need to be put in their places." Cindy was her usual all-business self and Tina looked very much like a lawyer, all self-control and polish. Nora felt anything but.

"I really don't think it's a good idea for me to be here. I'm not myself these days."

"Trust me Nora, none of us are ourselves. By the way, I like what you did to your hair."

Tina's clipped voice broke through Nora's thoughts.

"Uhm, thanks, I think," said Nora gulping. She had slept the entire day away, something unheard of for her. In her mad dash to get ready, Nora was lucky she had two matching high heels on. She hadn't bothered to check her hair. Her gut instinct told her that if she looked in a mirror she'd scream. The werecat she'd become last night had most definitely changed her. It would appear that change was both inside and out.

"I totally love the streaks of bright orange and black in it. It's very becoming," said Cindy.

"It's all natural." Nora gave a slightly terrified giggle, realizing instantly it sounded more like a purr than a slight laugh. She hoped her friends didn't notice. She let Tina lead the way. They claimed a table that was dead center. Both Cindy and Tina gave her a funny look as she covered her mouth.

"Wow, your voice sounded really sexy when you laughed. You should get a part-time job doing phone sex," teased Cindy.

"Thanks. Think I'll pass on that one," replied Nora, taking a seat next to Tina. Cindy claimed the other seat and leaned in closer to Nora.

"Your voice sounds like you're purring when you speak."

"What?" asked Nora, quickly adding, "That's insane...*pleeease,* people don't purr."

"You do," repeated Tina.

Luckily the three were forced to stop their bickering when the manager of the theatre Madam Sasha appeared at their side. She clutched a bright pink witch's hat in one hand and promptly placed it on Cindy's head.

"Thank you but I don't do hats." Cindy's words were a deadly zap of sarcasm.

"Ladies, I think you didn't read the sign when you walked in. Tonight, it's all about the magick. It's all about discovering your true potential, and letting the wild side out. That's why I called tonight "Your Magickal Wild Fantasy Night."

"Ohh, that's original."

Cindy wasn't normally rude to anyone. Nora watched her friend erratically pop a handful of colorful jellybeans into her mouth. *Something's up with her. At least she doesn't have to impress a goddess. What the heck am I thinking? At least she's a human and not some freaking werecat beast. Whatever's bothering her can't be half as serious as what I'm facing. And just where is the alcohol? I seriously need something to drink.*

"Come on gals. Be playful. The men love that. And, Cindy needs the sugar high, right, Cindy?" asked Sasha, moving the candy bowl closer to her friend.

Something is going on between those two. Nora watched the by-play between Cindy and Sasha and she vowed to get some answers later that night.

"You knew this would happen, didn't you?" asked Cindy to Sasha.

"No. Like my brother I had no idea when I first met you that you were—"

"A corporate climbing bitch."

Cindy's interruption caused Nora to roll her eyes.

"I take pride in calling myself a—"

"Look, Sasha aren't you supposed to be announcing the show? It's about to start." Tina's interruption was timed perfectly.

Gracefully, Sasha smiled. "Suits me. Let's get this show started." She turned and glided away. "See you later, sister-in-law."

Nora almost choked on the drink she'd grabbed from a nearby volunteer server.

"She's kidding," said Cindy quickly while shoving more jellybeans into her mouth.

"What did she mean by that?" asked Tina.

Cindy mumbled, "Nothing."

The stage lighting dimmed and Sasha took center stage. "Tonight, each of my special men will strut their assets alone and trust me, you won't be disappointed."

Tina fidgeted in her seat. "Alone."

"Assets," muttered Cindy.

"Special treat, my ass," snarled Nora.

The minute darkness settled on the crowd they all grew silent.

"Do you smell that?" Nora's nostrils flared, catching the distinctive odor of a female feline in heat. This time it wasn't her. She couldn't help the low growl that resonated from her.

"Shh," said her friends in unison.

The minute Hank stepped onto the stage, a dark hungering to rub her body up against his settled inside of Nora. She breathed deep...wrong move. His forest, Irish Spring soap scent caused her nipples to pucker into two tight buds and her panties immediately dampened as desire for Hank came hot and fast.

This was why she'd tried to get her friends to go to tonight's last blind date charity auction without her. Nora hoped to ignore her body's betrayal that was begging her to climb onto the stage and tear off Hank's clothing and do the dirty—not caring that a crowd was watching. She panted, feeling her panties dampen even more with cream.

"You okay, Nora?" asked Tina.

"Hey, what the hell's wrong with your eyes?" asked Cindy.

Nora was pleased Cindy's question diverted Tina because for the life of her she couldn't form a coherent thought. And that was wrong. The rational part of her that still existed told her she should run like the scaredy-cat she was, straight for the woods. *Maybe then the goddess Sakhmet, who I've pissed off, won't find me. As if.*

Nora got jarred out of her thinking when she heard the crowd's encouragement.

"Oh my god, he's stripping," laughed Tina.

"This is so good," drawled Cindy.

"This is not good at all," declared Nora, attempting to clamp her legs shut. Her pussy throbbed with desire and her skin had that hot, tingling sensation she got whenever she was about to change into her baser feline form. Then the ripe sex-scent of another feline snarled through her senses.

Attempting to zone in on the cat, Nora barely took her eyes off Hank, who was strutting to a wild, techno-jungle beat causing her heart to accelerate. Every single blasted button on his white shirt was now open, showcasing his lean, muscled abdomen, which had every woman in the hall oohing and ahhing for him. His hands played with his pant waistline, tugging them nice and low over his sleek hipbones.

Nora ground her teeth together and prayed to all the deities, gods and goddesses she'd ever heard about that he had better not be wearing some of those Velcro pants that could be whipped off lightning fast.

The second she heard the swooshing sound of Velcro being undone she cursed all said deities, gods and goddesses for not listening to her. With her eyes almost popping out of her head, Nora glared daggers at Hank. Then it dawned on her. Tonight, he wasn't wearing a mask. Tonight, it truly was Hank showcasing all his assets. But not for her alone.

The goddamn werecat was broadcasting loud and clear that he had a body most women would love to run their sleek palms over. Hank's slow striptease wasn't pleasing to Nora. Her palms were sweaty, her pussy pulsing and her nose kept twitching as she zeroed in on the other feline who was purring her own pleasure at Hank.

Finally finding her competition, Nora growled, not caring if anyone heard her. She forced herself to stop ogling Hank, who was currently wearing a tiger-striped thong. Then with a slow, torturous turn, all the women in the crowd saw his ass. *That ass is mine. He's sooo going to regret this.*

"Where are you going?" asked Tina.

"To kick some feline's butt," hissed Nora, pushing her chair out to make her way toward the other woman who was striding like an exotic panther to the stage.

Purposefully bumping into the woman with the long, sleek black hair, Nora flashed her teeth at her. "He's mine."

"Says who?" purred the woman.

Nora made sure the feline heard her low, vibrating growl that was laced with the threat of death. *Wow, when I get bitchy I go cat-bitchy all the way.*

A resonating rumble from the stage forced Nora's attention back to Hank. *Bad move again. That werecat has no shame.* Nora gulped hard and ran her sweaty palms over her jeans. Still moving his body in tune to the wild beat Hank was currently on his hands and knees, grinning, growling and flexing his hips up and down as he made his way to where Nora and her competition stood at the far-left side of the stage.

"I'm going to fuck him. You can't stop me."

This feline's confidence is going to be the death of her. What am I thinking? I'm a healer. I'm not some crazed cat that wants to fight for her mate.

"He's totally packed."

The woman's words rocked whatever sense Nora was holding on to off the ledge. "Packed," she muttered.

"You know, hung, loaded, cock-full."

The graphic terminology truly pissed off Nora.

"Ohh, yeah he's hung all right. And Kitten, that cock is all mine."

The woman, panther to the core, thought Nora, unsure how she knew that, turned and hissed at her. *Finally, I caught your attention.*

"By Sakhmet, who you calling Kitten? Cub."

The woman might as well be naked. She wore a slinky top, which dipped low enough to reveal her navel while showcasing her two large breasts.

Hank was grinning like a well-satisfied cat as he came nearer to them. "Ladies, no fighting."

Nora's competition flashed a pure fuck-me smile at Hank, ensuring his eyes caught the bouncy movement of her breasts. Nora quite literally saw red. The second before she felt that burning tingling feeling invade her body, Hank pulled her toward the lowering stage curtain.

Chapter Eight

Blood dripped down Nora's exposed arms. The panther-woman hadn't bothered with niceties after all. She'd gone all wild feline and Nora welcomed it.

The turn into the Royal Bengal Tiger that lived inside of Nora was fast and ferocious. She shook off the pain from the panther-woman who had attacked her noticing she had two huge claw-like gouge marks running down her arms. Somewhere in the back of her mind she knew Hank was watching. They had left the theater and found themselves shrouded in the darkness of the alley. Hank would not interfere. If he dared, Nora knew she'd kill him. This was her fight. This was something the cats that lived inside her said was hers by birth right.

That's how insanely base she'd become. The wild feline, the werecat she was had taken over. Nora roared, the sound loud with its own broadcast that she wasn't to be messed with. With her enhanced eyesight she watched the panther crouch, knowing the cat would aim for her throat. At the last second Nora turned her bulk to the right. The panther missed her by a millisecond, but it provided enough leverage for Nora to give a deadly slash to her competition. The panther hissed in pain. Nora didn't hesitate. With her other paw she slashed again. The last thing she expected was to be tackled from the back and thrown to the hard asphalt. The impact jarred her ribs. Scenting more than seeing the second panther, Nora forced herself to rebound quickly to her feet and shake off the stumble. Pain lanced her left side. A mental check revealed she had cracked a rib. With her breathing labored she stood strong and imposing, with all her teeth gleaming white against the black of the night.

So, you don't play fair. Nora forced the telepathic link into the panther-woman.

We are pride. We fight together and we fuck together.

Nora growled. She didn't like that answer and was pleased Hank was left out of the conversation because the woman Nora was knew *that* was every male's fantasy.

He will not interfere. The law says it so.

The law says one on one.

We are pride.

Nora didn't like their answers. She knew she was going to be left on her own. It was up to her to either embrace her true form, the werecat side, or die. *Nice reality check.* She braced for two frontal attacks.

Her eyes slanted to the right, following the slithering feline movements of the other panther-woman while maintaining eye contact with her true opponent.

They jumped her in unison. Nora's feet immediately braced for the impact. She tried turning to her left to avoid the head-on collision of the two large panthers coming straight for her face. The stark reality of what the panther-women were trying to inflict on Nora caused her to roar again. They weren't going to be happy simply killing her. No, they wanted to leave her face a horrific slash of claw marks.

A dark smoldering rage within Nora caused her breath to hitch. Panic that she was losing control of her reality, of the strange situation she currently found herself in, raised all the hairs on her body. In a blur of speed, she closed her eyes and gave into that deep, wild part of her she knew she had no control over. The cry of outrage that surged through the darkened alley caused both panthers to halt in their attack.

The transformation from the Royal Bengal Tiger into a prehistoric werecat, double the average size of the two panthers caused Nora to smile inwardly. She was sure, however, the werecat grin spreading across her feline face looked scary as hell. With her two long canine teeth dangling down past her mouth she knew she was a sight to be reckoned with.

Advancing in a slow gait, when in fact it was pure silent stealth, caused both panthers to make a hasty retreat.

Cowards. So much for fighting together! Nora pushed the thoughts like a deadly scratch straight into the panther-women and rejoiced when both screamed in agony.

Nice touch, Kitten.

Kitten? Who the hell is he calling Kitten? Nora swooped high and then low, gunning for Hank. If he knew what was good for him he'd turn and run. Instead, maintaining human form he stilled his movement, bending his tall frame into a crouching position. A second before her killer instinct kicked into high gear she slowed her crash-course into Hank's outstretched arms. He tugged on her head, weaving his hands into the thicket of her sable mountain lion coat. Gentle, lover-like hands caressed her still-quivering skin until a purr was evoked all on its own.

Turn.

His will she obeyed, breathing deep, pleased the transformation to human had healed her battered and cracked ribs. Then Hank stood, taking a step back.

Follow me. He turned, shredding his clothing in a quick flash of cells, morphing and turning into what he really was. What she really was. What they both were together. Darklander werecats to the core. He bounded away into the night. This time there was no thought when Nora gave into her true baser form. This time the turn was effortless, the power quickening her blood like a euphoric drug, enhancing all her senses. She knew instinctively where he was leading her. The forest—their own private bedroom.

The scrunch of the wet mulched ground was welcomed by the pads on the bottom of her paws. Her cells scented the pine, birch and hemlock trees once they had made their way to the heart of the forest that bordered the city. The sky was star-filled but cloudy. Her eyesight savored the night. In one blink, the heat of the forest animals and pulse of life was revealed as an inner eyelid clicked into place, showcasing a beautiful, vivid world, marked with hues of red, orange, green and yellow. The black of the night was simply a backdrop to the lush life that existed in the dark of the forest.

"Took you long enough." Naked, in human form with his cock protruding proud and thick before him stood Hank.

Nora turned, loving the cool caressing breeze sliding across her ultra-sensitive naked human skin. She didn't bother with the pretense of covering up her breasts. Instead, silent as the cats that lived within her she made a sultry move forward. Hank's eyes followed the bounce of her breasts. That one calculated glance on his part was enough to make Nora's pussy scream with desperate need. After all that had happened tonight she needed his cock crammed deep within her. He advanced, meeting her half way. No words were spoken. None were needed. The feline senses took stock of each other; each aware of the other's heightened arousal.

He pulled her tight to him, his fingers digging deep into the cups of her ass, ensuring she felt the throb of his erection up close and personal. She purred into him. Hank lowered his head a fraction of an inch. It was enough for Nora to latch onto his lips. With a growl of delight, she plunged her tongue deep into his mouth, mimicking what she wanted him to do with his cock to her cunt. Teeth clashed, each trying to dominate. His desperate need to get inside of her added the spark to her fire. Pushing her back onto the forest blanket, Nora eagerly accepted his weight on top of her.

Then in a flash of movement she reversed their roles. Tonight, she was the winner. Tonight, she was claiming her prize—Hank, her werecat, her mate. His green eyes flashed at her, welcoming her advances. Using her hands to hold Hank's arms down, Nora found what she wanted—his nipples. His back arched when she teased them both to dagger points. He growled and purred, bucking his hips up to meet the dew between her legs. Shamelessly, she rubbed her pussy back and forth over his cock, slicking him with her cream, marking him with her scent.

"Fuck me," growled Hank.

Park of Nora knew he was superior to her in strength and if he really wanted to take control of their positions he could. Because Hank was allowing her to have her way with him, she did as instructed.

Leveraging her dripping wet cunt above his thick, rock-hard cock, she lovingly impaled herself. Being stuffed with Hank's shaft was her ultimate reward. She moved up and down, riding him and grinding against him like a hellcat. Nora thrust with all she had each time, sliding dangerously close to the edge of bliss. Hank's hands clawed at her ass then moved to her hips, allowing him to set the pace. She welcomed it. Throwing back her head, she mewed as his skillful fingers found her nub. Hank flicked her pebbled pearl back and forth, and the flash of the orgasm that tore through Nora's body had her grinding hard onto his cock and fingers. Vaguely Nora felt Hank's body meet her through the cloudy, languid feeling as she came back from bliss to earth.

Hank rubbed her back, allowing her to purr into the aftershocks of their sizzling sex. She moved her legs to curl around his waist. He flipped her over, her back welcoming the cool of the forest blanket.

"Now, I plan to make love to you."

Really, he didn't need to say that but like always Hank continually surprised her. He'd long ago shed the masks he wore and now he lay bare to her, his feelings written clearly through the longing in his emerald green eyes.

Could I love him? Do I love him? Those two thoughts clashed into Nora. The reality was she did. When that had happened, she had no idea. Vaguely she thought she'd loved him from that first night and that scared her. *Love at first sight.* The idea was slightly fanciful, full of some young girl's dream for a knight in shining armor. She giggled. Hank was anything but a knight. More the steed, the beast, that would come in to slash the foe.

"Do you accept what you are?"

The sensual cadence of the voice caused a chill of goose bumps to form over Nora's skin. Sakhmet. The Goddess Sakhmet stood in front of them in her elegant, casual pose about to set her judgment.

Fear leashed tight, catching Nora's heart, making it impossible to speak.

"Cat got your tongue?"

Humor? Tell me she did not crack a joke.

"You honor us with your presence, goddess, but the day is not over."

"I would choose my words carefully, Hank. Your lives are getting short."

Hank wisely bowed his head, letting the air of silence reign.

With shaky legs, Nora stood up, making sure to give a quick bow to the goddess. "I accept what I truly am." The minute she said the words she knew them to be true. A breath of air escaped her and she smiled.

Sakhmet bowed her head. "It pleases me well to see you embrace the blessing gift I have bestowed on you. Honor this gift, human, with reverence and you will honor yourself, Hank and your blessed offspring."

"Offspring?" squeaked Nora, silently saying a prayer she was not pregnant. *And just what would I deliver? A baby or kittens?*

Sakhmet smiled, the yellow of her eyes casting an eerie glow to the cloudy night. "Your thoughts are amusing. Werecats deliver babies but if you'd like I could bequeath you with kittens."

Nora shook her head. "No thanks. When I'm ready to have a baby, I'd like it to have fingers and toes instead of paws and claws."

"Then it shall be so. Honor your mate well, Hank and I will be gentle when next you pass into the Darklander fade."

Nora hadn't heard Hank come to stand beside her, not that his stealth approach shocked her anymore. He linked his fingers through hers but bobbed his head again in Sakhmet's direction. "Thank you."

The goddess bowed her head slightly and then in a fast cat-blink she was gone. The wind, which had stilled to the goddess' commands, breathed its way through the forest, caressing Nora's skin. She shivered.

Taking her arm in his, Hank said, "I know just the thing to warm you up."

Together they silently made their way through the forest back to Nora's home. "We can keep walking in human form and this will take an hour or turn into our feline forms and be there in ten minutes."

Nora liked that Hank was asking her permission, giving her the choice to turn into the werecat she was.

"That would be great. The quicker we get home the warmer I'll be."

"Trust me once we're in your house you'll be toasty warm after I'm through with you."

"Is that a promise?"

"No, it's absolute certainty," he squeezed her hand; a surge of warmth teased its way through her cells. "And the minute we're home I plan to make love to you in every way."

"Every way?" Her breath came out as a sigh.

Hank leaned into her. "Kitten, every way."

"Promises, promises," she purred, insuring he felt the seductive rub of her skin as she turned into her true werecat form.

A heart-beat later Hank followed suit brushing against her. They teasingly raced through the forest's canopy of trees, each eager for the cradle of a bed so they could create their own hellcat style of loving.

Don't miss out!

Visit the website below and you can sign up to receive emails whenever Renee Field publishes a new book. There's no charge and no obligation.

https://books2read.com/r/B-A-HRN-PPOR

BOOKS 2 READ

Connecting independent readers to independent writers.

Did you love *Be My Werecat Tonight*? Then you should read *Be My Vampire Tonight*[1] by Renee Field!

Bidding on a masked man at an auction is all for a good cause, but what happens when he turns out to be a vampire who has the power to unleash the wild woman lying dormant inside you?

As a Darklander vampire, Mitch has spent a century living in a bleak world, but all that changes when he sees Tina. The beast living within Mitch wants to stake his claim. Mitch knows taking Tina's virginity will change her forever, but try explaining that to a woman whose passion cannot be denied.

Tina holds the key to his freedom, but Mitch will be damned forever before he turns her over as a slave for his master.

Book one in the Darklander Lovers series.

---

1. https://books2read.com/u/3RoMDG

2. https://books2read.com/u/3RoMDG

Read more at www.reneefield.com.

Also by Renee Field

A Warriors of Maida Novella
Love Me Wild
Love Me Tender
Love Me Strong
Love Me Wild

Darklander Lovers
Be My Warlock Tonight
Be My Vampire Tonight
Be My Werecat Tonight

Elemental Love
Heart of Mine

Riverton Cove series
Embrace

Titan series
Rapture
Bliss

Standalone
Claiming A Siren's Heart
Claiming Poseidon's Heart
A Siren's Wish
Fairy Cursed
Summer Heat
Queen of Dragons
Summer Heat
Electrify Me

Watch for more at www.reneefield.com.

About the Author

Renee loves to write a variety of genres. She writes for HQN Spice Briefs and also writes sensual paranormal romance, and contemporary romance as an Indie author. Field also writes nitty gritty young adult and paranormal young adult romance novels under the pen name Renee Pace. Renee calls Halifax, Nova Scotia, Canada home and loves her view of the Atlantic Ocean. She is a member of Romance Writers' of America, and her local Romance Writers of Atlantic Canada. She juggles work, four children and is a firm believer in soul-mates and the power of the sea.

Renee loves to hear from fans. She can be reached by email at reneefieldauthor@gmail.com

Read more at www.reneefield.com.